LA CUCARACHA
&
OTHER TALES
OF
APOCALYPTIC REVELRY

Written by
Michael Dominguez-Beddome

Illustrations By
Kevin Budnik

Cover and Illustrations by Kevin Budnik - http://kevinbudnik.com

Edited by Mary Hennicke and Michel Dominguez-Beddome

Disclaimer: This is a work of fiction. Names, characters, businesses, places, events and incidents are either the products of the author's imagination or used in a fictitious manner. Any resemblance to actual persons, living or dead, or actual events is purely coincidental.

ISBN: 1-946845-02-7
ISBN-13: 978-1-946845-02-3

MichaelDominguezBeddome.com

This book is for everyone who sees life in black and white. May your vision clear up soon! There're so many wonderful things to see in the world.

Prologue:

"Explosive Tantrums
&
Birthday Fiascos"

*Pre Structured Railroad Time — Yucatan,
Mexico*

"**M**om! Mom! Mom! Mom! Mom! Mommy! MOMMM!" Babysaurus shouted at Mommysaurus as he jumped up and down on their designer chiropractor-approved Stone Number Bed, excited for the big day — and before you ask, all the numbers were the same: *100*, unless you foraged for leaves or something, but who needs the work?

Mommy opened her eyes and sighed heavily, rolling onto her side and grabbing at Daddy's neck with her teeth, so he would make the kid breakfast. She needed five more minutes.

Daddysaurus had resigned himself to this duty. It was easier this way than debating the subject. He'd end up losing anyway. The weary Alamosaurus dad rolled his giant flabby body from the smooth slab and dragged his now five-year-old son from the room before his wife had a fit.

"So kiddo, what do you want to do today?" Daddy poured a bowl of Lawnio's® Full O' Fiber® Cereal and sat down next to the 10-ton creature who had already begun devouring the roughage-based breakfast product. Between bites Baby spouted, "Bounce...House!...Fútbol...game!...See...Cousin!"

"That's a lot of great ideas. But just so you know, I have a very special birthday plan for you!" Daddy said with a coy grin.

"Does... Mommy... know?" Baby asked.

"...Not as of yet. But she will!"

"Mommy's... in... charge... Daddy. Don't... make... her... angry... on... my... birth... day."

"How very observant you are... Well I'm sure she'll be thrilled. I've been planning it for ages."

"Should've... told... Mommy... ages... ago... then..."

"Shouldn't have told you at all I suppose."

"Suppose... so." Baby swallowed his food.

"Finish up little one, and get dressed. You need to pack a sweater, it could be breezy where we're going."

"Yay!"

The kettle screamed and Daddy swiveled his neck to take the kettle off the stove.

Mommy entered looking like an entirely new saurus.

"Good morning my little sunshine! My five year old Baby!"

Baby drank the rest of the grassy milk in the bowl and said, "Morning, Mommy! Daddy has plans he'd like to discuss with you while I pack my sweater for our breezy trip somewhere! Bye!"

Baby jumped to his feet and bounded to his bedroom, giggling.

"Plans? Breezy trip? I thought we were going to see Baby's Grammy? That's what we had discussed."

"Yeah that's what we had discussed. And we will. First stop."

"Where are you planning on going?" she asked.

Daddy took a teabag and plunged it into the boiling water to ponder his words.

"So here's..." Daddy took a sip: not steeped enough, too bitter.

"...What I'm thinking. You know my favorite guy from the self help carvings I've been trying to show you?"

"We're not going to a rally or something? The kid is five, not fifty."

"No we're not going to a rally. Today... He had mentioned in his last series that there'd be a fireworks show over the Gulf tonight so I figured what better way to spend the kid's birthday then with fireworks?"

"The Gulf is three hours away," Mommy said flatly.

"Well, and this is actually a little further. They're setting off out by Chicxulub."

"You gotta be kidding. I know the water's pretty but the kid can barely make it 523 LatSecs before he starts whining."

"Yeahhhh, it's about 1193 LatSecs... so there's that."

"Not gonna happen. Sorry. Nice thought, but wholly impractical." Mommy walked out of the room to check on Baby and took all the air in the room with her.

But Daddy wasn't going to be shut down so easily. This had been stewing in his mind for months. Ever since he heard about the festivities at the Oracle Epoch's speech downtown, he knew this was the perfect way to ring in the kid's fifth birthday. He had to figure it out. And then he did.

"Daddy, we're ready to go to Grammy's! Where are you?" Baby was wearing some trendy shorts with a matching collared shirt that Mommy picked out, and Mommy was wearing the matching Mommy-version of the same get-up. They looked around the house, calling his name until Daddy shouted, "Baby! Come out back!"

Baby ran out the back door of the house and found Daddy strapped into a clumsy looking device of his own making. It was a sort of chariot—the body was made from a bunch of fern branches tied hastily together to make a sled, with two long sturdy wooden handles pulled up over Daddy's shoulders and tied to his neck with many meters worth of roots and vines.

"Hop in, Baby! We're going to the beach!"

"Mommy, yay! The beach, Mommy! Is Grammy coming too? I so wanted to see Grammy!"

Mommy gave Daddy the death stare. "Yes Daddy, is Grammy coming? You know how she can't walk very far these days? How will she be joining us?"

Daddy took a deep breath. "I've got a plan for that too."

"Yayyyyyy!" Baby cheered as he ran around the yard, frolicking and trampling other smaller dinosaurs that were picking at the flowerbed like it was a breakfast buffet.

"Yeahhh yayyy! So, let's get a move on you two. Daddy needs to scavenge for more ferns at Grammy's."

Baby hopped in the chariot, and Mommy tied him in with roots, and the three of them travelled up the long road to Grammy's town one hour north of them.

*****

Grammysaurus was standing on the porch, as the family pulled up in front. Baby was over the moon, and ripped through his roots to hug her. Daddy was thrilled to be free for a second—for a five-year-old, this kid was damn heavy.

"Hey Gram," Daddy muttered through labored breaths.

"Daddy." She responded without the same warmth.

Daddy and Grammy had a bit of a strained relationship since Daddy and Grampysaurus had a duel a few years back, resulting in the eventual bleed out and total body carnage of Grampy. It didn't help that it was on Grammy and Grampy's anniversary, but Grampy challenged Daddy, not the other way around. That's how Daddy saw it anyway.

Mommy and Baby went inside with Grammy, while Daddy began his search for more branches.

"So you're how old now? Four?" Grammy asked, already knowing the answer.

"Five, Grammy! I'm five!"

"Five! Oh my goodness! How big you are! Well Grammy got you a nice birthday present fit for a big boy!"

She went into her cupboard and pulled out a box wrapped in maple leaves, and tied up with vines, and handed it to her grandson. Baby jumped up and down at the sight of it. He tore the leaves to shreds with his teeth and flung open the box to find a Baby-sized telescope, only ten feet long.

"What is it, Grammy?"

"It's a spy glass, little one! You look through the one side here, and it shows you stuff far away from the other side! You'll need someone to help you hold it of course, but it should give you hours of fun! My Daddy gave me one just like it when I was your age. Though this one's a little bit more advanced."

"Wow! What do you say, Baby?" said Mommy, impressed with the gift herself.

"Thank you, Grammy! I love it!"

"You're welcome little Baby, I hope you enjoy it."

She hugged him close.

"Where'd your father get to? He looks like he's seen better days," Grammy stated without too much concern.

"He's got a plan for today," Mommy said, rolling her eyes.

7

"Ahh a plan. *Men with plans.* What is it, did he tell you?"

Mommy leaned in and spoke into Grammy's ear out of earshot of Baby, while Baby jumped up and down trying to hear. "What is it? What is it? What is it?"

"Just a second, Baby." Mommy sighed and turned back to her mother.

"That's nice of him, leaving dear old Grammy out in the rain. He does remember I can't make it that far, doesn't he? What an ass."

"He said he has a plan for that too," Mommy replied.

"Baby, come here a minute. Listen good, okay? When you get married..."

"Married!? Ickkky Grammy!"

"Yes, Icky Grammy, but someday, but when you get married, do not *ever* make plans. Understand? *Mommies* make plans, *Daddies* carry them out. That's the way of the world. You know what that sign there says?" She gestured to a wooden sign over the doorframe, with words painted in berries across the front.

"No."

"It says, 'Happy Wife, Happy Life.' You understand?"

"Yes, Grammy."

"Good. Go find your Daddy while Mommy and I catch up a little."

"Okay."

Baby ran out the front onto the porch and looked both directions. About a LatSec down the road, Baby saw Daddy hacking off the better part of a tree. "Daddy what are you doing?"

"Stay there Baby, I'm coming back." Daddy dragged an enormous pile of greenery back up the street to the porch. "Wanna help your Daddy build a project?"

Baby came off the porch and looked at the greenery.

"What do we do?" Baby asked.

"Follow my lead here. It's a bit of a guess and check."

Daddy looked back at the chariot from earlier, and dragged branches to the correct places, and Baby held them down while Daddy tied them together with vines and roots.

After a good thirty minutes, Chariot 2.0 was complete. It was about 13 meters long, with branches woven in and out of each other in a fairly sturdy looking pattern. As Daddy crunched the last of the seams together with pine sap, Mommy and Grammy came out onto the porch to see where the men had gotten to.

"What's going on out here, kids?" Mommy asked.

"We're building Grammy a cart like mine!"

"HA, good luck if you think you're getting me on that rickety death trap."

"Grammy we built it for you."

"Yeah Grammy, you're not going to ditch your grandson on his birthday are you? When Baby worked oh so hard so you can come?" Daddy smiled an evil smile at Grammy.

"Ohhh well played son-in-law, well played." Grammy sighed and forced a smile. "Of course I'm coming Baby! I wouldn't miss your big day for the world. And if I should die in transit, just know that your daddy cares more about saving himself from your Mommy's noose than he does about federal regulations for pedestrian-powered vehicles. Who's ready for a road trip?"

"Yayyyy!" Baby jumped onto his little cart. Mommy climbed up front, and Daddy tied them both in together. Then Grammy hobbled onto her cart, and Daddy tried to strap her in before she smacked him on the cheek and did it herself. Mommy tied the cart to Daddy's neck and shoulders. And they were off again. Slower this time. If Baby was heavy before, add 35 tons and a penchant for backseat driving.

"Only 2/3 of the trip to go!" Daddy took deep breaths and dreamed about the Oracle Epoch. *This kid is going to love this. If it's the last thing he does, this will wow him.*

*****

After three hours in heavy traffic, and yes there was traffic—big community events at rush hour always have traffic—they could finally see the beach! Grammy's butt had gone numb from sitting but her tail could feel the burn as it dragged underneath the rapidly eroding fern chariot. Baby had long fallen asleep, and Mommy wasn't thrilled with Daddy's unilateral road trip plans and by extension Daddy in general right now. So Daddy was alone with his thoughts.

I wonder if the Oracle Epoch is going to be there. That would be so cool! Not that Baby will care. Or the ladies. But he's usually pretty good at predicting exciting happenings. Like didn't he predict that weird metallic machine landing smack dab in town square with some big headed green dudes called Marshall, and other weird looking two-legs came to town for a bit before realizing they couldn't get a mortgage in this economy and left? I think that was Epoch. Either way, it's hard to find a reliable Oracle in this day and age. Used to be such a common career choice. I blame lackadaisical parenting. But on the other hand, maybe those Marshalls were on to something when they left. If the housing market is such crap, why would anyone gamble on a degree in Prophecy when you have to provide for your kids? Where is the joy in the world now? We tell our kids they can do anything, but they come out of school overeducated and thoroughly over-debted for this anachronistic agricultural world. My schooling was a tenth the cost of tuition nowadays. Well not my son! He's going to actually do whatever he wants. I'm going to open him a savings account...

"Daddy!"

Daddy snapped back to reality. "Yes Baby, what's up?"

"I gotta pee!"

"Ok baby, Mommy we gotta stop."

"You don't have to fight me to get a break."

They unstrapped Baby and Grammy, and Baby and Daddy went behind a patch of about seven or eight trees so Baby could have privacy.

"How you doing, Gram?" Mommy asked, cracking her shoulders and stretching out her neck.

"About as good as an old lady can riding on top of a moving arboretum. I think I have a hive up my keister."

"At least you get to ride. Baby may look cute, but he ain't light anymore."

"Well he was big when he was born. Biggest egg of the bunch if I remember right."

"Yeah," Mommy mumbled, as though she could forget.

"Be grateful he's the only one that survived, can you imagine dragging three kids in that shoddy piece of work? I told you you should've married that engineer. At least even if he was a schmuck, he'd be able to build a *proper* cart for his wife to haul around like a common laborer."

"There's nothing wrong with hard work, mother."

"There's nothing wrong with dinner at Grammy's too. And yet here we are, you slaving away, and me wondering how I'll make a reservation for my proctologist with one day's notice—he fills up quick you know."

Mommy burst into laughter.

"What's so funny?"

"Nothing mother." She tried to reel it back in and take a deep breath.

"Tell me dammit, I only got so much time left on this rock, I could use a laugh."

"Fine. Hah. Fine. Ok. Your proctologist fills up quick, aye?"

"I don't get your observation."

"Never mind."

"Explain this to me, maybe I'm not so fast on the uptake."

"He's a nice doctor... *butt* man is he rough to get it in with."

"Right, he books up usually a week ahead. That's my point."

"Mine too."

"Okay then."

"Great. Leaving it there then."

"How far are we, Mommy?" Daddy called from behind the bush.

Mommy finally stifled her giggles. She raised her neck to full apex and looked out over the city traffic.

"Looks like a half an hour or so. Thank the lord. If Daddy's right, the fireworks show is just after the sun sets, and that doesn't give us much time here."

"Are we just going to the beach? If this is the big display—where did he hear about this? That Oracle Epoch guy? What a quack!—how are we going to find seats? I bet it fills up before we arrive."

"Very possible," Mommy suddenly realized.

"I'm going to get strapped back into this deathtrap so we can get a move on. Don't want the kid having to sit on your or, god forbid, *my* shoulders when we get there."

"He'd never sit on your shoulders Grammy. He'd sit on Daddy's."

"Daddy's going to need to see a doctor after this is over too... I ain't no supermodel. I can eat."

"DADDY! TIME TO GO!" Mommy yelled to the bush.

"ONE MORE MINUTE!" He shouted, then whispered, "Stay right here buddy."

Daddy came round from the bush and whispered to Mommy, "Baby had a little accident, do we have spare undies?"

"I think we do, lemme see." Mommy turned back to the cart where the luggage was tied. "Daddy, where is the luggage?"

"It's on the cart, it should be on your cart...which it's *not*...fantastic."

"It's gone?"

"I'm sure it's not gone, I'm sure it's just a bit up the road, let me go look."

Daddy hobbled back up the road at a quickened pace, shaking the ground with every step. After ten minutes, Daddy returned without any luck.

"We gotta go, where is it?" Mommy asked.

"It's gone. And the sun is setting. Baby! It's time to come out of the bush, Daddy's gonna fix this in his own way."

"How's that? Naturism is forbidden outside of the mountain towns," Grammy cracked. Daddy gave her a look and removed his top shirt. "I'm sure this will be a little big on you kiddo, but we gotta keep going if we're going to see the fireworks."

Daddy laced the t-shirt onto Baby's legs and Baby came out dragging half a ton of fabric behind him.

"It's so heavy!" Baby broke down in tears, feeling humiliated and tired from the trip. Mommy scooped him onto the cart, strapped him in and pet his head with hers. "It's okay little one. Guess what today is?"

"My...birth...day!" Baby said through sobs.

"That's right, you're my big little Baby today, and we got a great surprise waiting for you on the beach, so don't worry, Mommy's going to get you there and Daddy's going to find you new undies when we get there. Okay sweetie?"

"O...kay!" Baby sobbed a bit more, but could see the light at the end of the tunnel, until the news just hit him: "But... I'm...so...tired!" Baby broke down again. Daddy and Mommy strapped themselves back in.

"It's okay little one, Grammy's here with you." Grammy pet his head with hers as well, and soothed his spirit. Then calmly whispered to Mommy and Daddy, "Time to get to the beach. Now."

The two of them took off at a soft jog. They knew they had to hurry to make it in time, and after everything they've been through, that was the only option. As they hustled down the streets, they knocked smaller dinosaurs over with their ground thuds, and as they got close to the beach, Daddy heard a sound he was hoping he'd never hear again: police. He turned around and saw a smaller dino cop chasing after them in full uniform, making whining siren noises with his mouth. "Mommy, get there, we'll be right behind you," Daddy said to her.

He stopped suddenly and spun himself horizontally to block the street with his body so the officer couldn't chase Mommy instead.

The cop came to a stop, and removed his helmet, approaching Daddy and Grammy.

"Hi officer, what's the problem?" Daddy said hurriedly.

"Firstly, your tone."

"Sorry, I meant, 'Is there a problem officer?'"

"Correct question. Yes there is a problem; you were speeding! Your driving was reckless and there seem to be several dinosaurs left in your wake!"

"Officer, I know how this looks," as he looked back at the line of downed carts and light posts, "but honestly, we're in a very big hurry!"

"Oh you're in a hurry. That makes it all fine then doesn't it?"

"No you don't understand, see..."

"Officer!" Grammy chimed in and leaned over to the cop. "Officer please, every second we're here is another second of my agony!"

"I don't follow," asked the cop, now nervous for her sake. "Are you hurt?"

"Hurt? In a way, yes. I'm about to lay eggs!"

"You are??" Daddy and the Officer both shouted in disbelief before Daddy understood and corrected his statement with a, "you are."

"That's right officer, we need to get to the hospital!"

"Well this is highly irregular..."

"You're telling me, I thought I was barren, but here we are! Let us pass please!"

"You from 'round here?"

"Not really," Grammy said.

"I'll take you to the hospital myself then!"

"Oh joy." Daddy replied with a forced smile.

"Come on!" The officer put on his helmet again, and took off at a jog and started his siren whine again.

Daddy whispered to Grammy, "Thank you, that was quick thinking."

"It's all for Baby, kid. Nobody puts Baby in a cop cart. Now step on it!"

Daddy and Grammy followed the cop to the hospital.

16

Meanwhile Mommy and Baby kept their pace. They just had to get to the beach before the fireworks started. The sun was almost set.

Just a few more blocks and they'd be there.

Mommy came around the corner and saw a crazy line of dinosaurs also trying to get to the shore. They wouldn't make it. Mommy considered her options. To her side, she noticed a multistory building and decided she'd put Baby up on the roof. Best view of anybody up there. She lifted the small child with her teeth and plopped him down atop the roof, leaning in with her head so she could keep him warm.

"Did we make it?" Baby asked, now mostly calm.

"We made it."

Music began to play and the Oracle Epoch came out onto a stage on the beach to the applause of the attendees.

"Thank you all for coming tonight! It is my pleasure and honor to present you with the Chicxulub Chamber Orchestra who will be accompanying the light show this evening." The dinosaurs clapped politely.

"For those of you who know me, thank you for coming to the summer edition of the Concert on the Beach series that we like to put on every few months. For those of you who don't know who I am, my name is Epoch Chopra. I am an oracle, author, speaker, life planner and lover of all things arts and culture. I'm so glad to be able to share with you the events of the evening. First up, the Chicxulub Chamber Orchestra will play a beautiful piece delivered to us by the two-legged Marshall family from out of town just a little time ago. The Marshall's have proven invaluable to this year's concert season, supplying a number of orchestral masterpieces including the first piece which you will hear tonight, called the "1812 Overture" by another two-legger named Pyotr Ilyich Tchaikovsky. The finale will bring with it the celestial fireworks I've promised you all. I hope you enjoy it. Thank you for joining us tonight."

"Where's Daddy and Grammy?" asked Baby.

Mommy didn't really know what to say. She didn't want to let her son down on his birthday, but didn't want to lie either.

"Well son..." She looked for words. But instead saw Daddy's head coming up the block from behind the shorter dinosaurs.

"They're here." She smiled. Daddy stopped the cart and hugged Mommy. They propped Grammy up in front of them so she could see the show.

"Daddy, hand this to Baby." Grammy lifted a small kale cake out of her bag, slightly smooshed but mostly in tact, and handed it to Daddy, who in turn put it down in front of Baby.

"Happy birthday kiddo."

"Happy birthday Baby!"

"Happy birthday son."

The four of them group-hugged as the song began. As the minutes went by, a bright ball in the sky appeared, and drew closer and closer.

"Oooo pretty!" Baby said as he munched down on his cake. He pulled the telescope out that Grammy had given him and watched the ball fall to Earth magnificently alight.

"It is pretty isn't it?" Asked Mommy.

"Not as pretty as Mommy." Replied Daddy.

"Okay you softies, the fireworks are coming, don't ruin it!" said Grammy.

As the song came to a climax, the ball from the sky struck the sea behind them with tremendous force in a blinding and beautiful flash, causing a giant tsunami, among other things, to head straight for them. The orchestra players stood from their seats and bowed with their instruments held over their hearts. As they stood upright, the volcanoes surrounding the beach all erupted violently as well. It was a coordinated light show, if ever they saw one. The fiery lights drew closer to the beach, glassing nearby sandbars en route. The tsunami grew ever larger, flooding over the smaller islands entirely. The projectile lava flew into the sky and blocked out the sun. If the Chicxulub Gazette reporters were to describe it, they would call the show, "A dramatic triumph!"—that is, if they could survive the most explosive classical beach concert the world had ever known.

"By the way, Baby, I got you fresh undies at the hospital!" said Daddy.

"The hospital?" asked Mommy.

"Long story," Grammy said.

"Thank you, guys. This has been the best birthday ever!"

Grammy smiled. "Here's to many more!"

"La Blancocabra"

Late February, 1519 — Yucatan, Mexico

"Y̶ou're *sure* sure? Like, we won't look like idiots if this doesn't come to pass?" The Chief looked the Vizier dead in the eye.
"Yeah totally, I'm definitely totally *sure* sure."

"What makes you so sure this time? Remember the last time you were pretty dang sure? We had that neighborhood picnic, and they didn't end up coming and we had to toss out a crap ton of elotes, not to mention the homemade salsa from those northern Algonquians. Man, we got in trouble for that one. You know how much wastefulness irks the modern voter... think about disgusting buffalo tongues for goodness sakes."

"I promise, I'm pretty damn sure this time."

"Again, let me impress upon you the importance here. People will come from all around. And again I ask for proof: what makes you so sure? Don't just tell me you're optimistic, 'cause I'm not, frankly. I want stone cold evidence, proof, likely clues, etc. So make with the proof."

The Vizier hated this. He sighed, rubbing the sweat from his forehead with his left hand. *No one seems to trust me anymore... you make one shoddy guess...* "Uhhh, okay, concrete proof is what you want."

"Yes, thank you. Proceed," demanded the Chief, as he sat back on his spinal shaped throne. "You, slave, I'm a little too warm for comfort, please fix that."

A P.O.W from a neighboring tribe hobbled over to his throne and lifted a small skull from behind the boney seat. The hollowed cap was full of a bubbling stockpile of fresh, but now cooled blood and a small name-brand basting brush. He lifted the brush from the vessel and began to paint the chilled liquid onto the back of the Chief's neck, and immediately the breeze blowing through the elaborate throne room caught the moisture and he was relieved. "Oh yeah, that's the stuff... thanks, you're good."

The P.O.W bowed and took his position behind the Vizier. The Vizier proceeded to fumble through his tablets, mumbling indistinctly to himself while he searched for a specific document.

"Well?" asked the Chief growing impatient.

"Here it is." The Vizier sighed with relief. "Here it is, Your Majesty! This is your proof." He handed the stone tablet to his ruler and bowed backwards to give him space to review it. The Chief sat up in his chair, his eyes scoured the words written therein, and after a few moments turned to the Vizier.

"Oy, come here."

"Me sir?" asked the Vizier. The Chief looked at him and furrowed his brows.

"Yessir, coming, no problem." The advisor double timed it up to the throne and sat to the Chief's right side.

"So what the hell am I looking at? There's obviously a lot going on here. I didn't really feel like reading a novel today, give me the bullet points."

"Uhh right, of course. If you look here, you'll notice the prophecy has foretold the arrival of a pale collective of lispy seafarers. From a place called... the Siberian Peninsula."

"Uh huh, go on, I know that part."

"Well if you look several lines lower, you'll notice it mentions the golden rule of our forefathers: "fooleth me once, shameth on thee; fooleth me twice, shameth on me."

"And?"

"And? Isn't it clear? The Prophets of Old knew that one day we would be fooled once, and much food and many miles walked would be wasted. Voters were always going to be pissed before the real deal came on the scene, how else would true excitement be stirred?"

"So what you're saying is, because the earth deities tricked us last time, and the Algonquians trekked for six months to be here, we are now worthy of our lispy guests?"

"Exactly!"

The Chief stared at the tablet. The room was silent—everyone grew deathly nervous that there would be a murdered advisor anytime, because how stupid was that prediction?! Who would fall for such an ambivalent and tenuous predic...

"Brilliant!" shouted the Chief. "Let's get it going, begin all preparations. Send word to our neighbors and friends from all around, that this time, it's really game time. Even bigger than before. There'll be fireworks, and a fountain of blood in the town square... actually get an estimate on that one—I don't know if that's a really good idea in this heat, but see how much it'll cost because it could be a nice bit of spectacle if we get a reasonable price. Also, see if that traveling zoo would make an appearance—I bet our pale guests would love to see those dancing Chupacabra you set up for my birthday last year."

"Excellent, I'll begin at once." The Vizier sighed with relief and bowed to the Chief before exiting hastily. The P.O.W scoffed. *He's insane! What kind of idiot would believe such things?*

"What is it, slave?" The P.O.W snapped out of his daze and looked at the Chief who glared at him. P.O.W shook his head adamantly. *Did I say that out loud? Oh crap...*

"I see that look on your face, slave." *Oh, thank the lord!*

"Do you disapprove?"

"Disapprove, sir? Who am I to think anything?"

"Good. That's what *I* thought, but I'm glad you agree. I'm going to take a walk, why don't you take thirty and stretch your legs?"

"Cool... that sounds good sir," said the P.O.W in shock.

"Shut up and go, I don't know what to do with you really. I preferred the other girl... whatshername... fan boy, what's the slave girl's name again? Mallory, Malvina...."

"Malinalli, sir?" suggested the fan boy.

"Malinalli! That's it. I liked her better, but the wife didn't want her around, so I'm stuck with you. So, go make yourself busy... or whatever. Read a book, or something. I'll send for you when I'm back."

"Very good."

"Of course very good. Get out."

The P.O.W shut up at last and bowed, then made a beeline for the exit.

The Chief sat down again.

"What was I doing again?... Oh right! Walking! Nah, forget it. Fan boy, tell me a story."

*****

The Vizier made quick work of alerting the town, and set out to notify the neighboring tribes. As he made his way to the town's edge, he noticed the

P.O.W meandering willy nilly along the forest's periphery and ran to him.

"You!" screamed the Vizier. The P.O.W panicked and turned into a tree smacking his forehead on a lower branch. He grabbed his nose and held his face, trying to rub away the stinging the bark caused. "Owwww."

"What the hell do you think you're doing?" questioned the Vizier.

"Me? I'm just kinda walking. The Chief made me leave and it's too early to have a pulque," *Though it's five o'clock somewhere,* the P.O.W thought, but then continued, "So I'm just getting a little exercise I suppose. Not as fun I know, but..."

"So he knows you're here?"

"Well not here exactly, but he knows I'm not there."

"Okay, and you don't have anything to do?"

"Not really. I'm not from here, so people aren't exactly lining up to invite me over for a BBQ..."

"I didn't ask for your life story. The festival is coming and I need a hand with preparations."

"Ohh okay. What can I help you with?"

"Alright here's my list. I already hung invite-banners around town. I still need to contact the following vendors, and alert the Nahuas and the Aztecs about the party."

"No Olmecs? No Inca?" asked the P.O.W.

"No. Last time the Olmecs trashed the place, and the Inca couldn't make the trip—too far—so I don't want to waste manpower inviting them when they're never gonna come anyway."

"Ahh."

"So, what do you want to start with?" the Vizier asked, grateful to have a helper.

It struck the P.O.W that the Vizier is a few stars short of a constellation, given his latest idiotic prediction, but... it couldn't be this easy...

"Well, I'm a fast runner, I did track in school. Let me deliver your invitation to the Nahuas and the Aztecs. I have a Nahua cousin anyway, and she can help spread the word."

"Yes! That's exactly what I need. This party needs to go off without a hitch if our re-election campaign will be a success. Here's a few dozen invites," the Vizier handed the P.O.W a backsack filled with about thirty stone tablets with the date and the address, almost knocking him over. "Please be quick about it though... I want RSVPs so I can finalize orders with the vendors."

"Yeah great, of course. RSVPs for you and me's." The P.O.W smiled; shocked that this was going to work.

"I like your enthusiasm, kid. What's your Nahua cousin's name? I travel there a lot, maybe I know her."

"Uhh her name's... Jane... Jane Llorona." Since Malinalli just escaped from the clutches of the palace herself, the P.O.W wasn't about to give him her real first name, or he'd never be allowed to leave.

"Hmmm, doesn't ring a bell. Oh well, hop to it. Can't wait to hear back!"

"Me neither!"

The two smiled at each other genuinely. This was going to be the Vizier's big break, and the P.O.W's big break for it. What's not to love?

They parted ways and the Vizier ran to the small business camp on the other side of town to find a lowly craftsman to get a fountain estimate.

*****

Meanwhile aboard a large craft one hundred miles out to sea, Hernan Cortes was looking nervously off the bow of his... I won't say stolen, as he wouldn't use that word... *liberated* Cuban ship. The navigator tapped Cortes on the shoulder and he turned to him frantically.

"What!?"

"You've been so tense, sir, come down from there. I made up a nice hammock in the front of the ship for you; I put out the book from your nightstand. The sun is shining, and a lovely cross breeze is blowing. Please, enjoy the day. Your pacing is making the crew very nervous."

"Well why shouldn't they be nervous for Christsakes? The Cuban settlement is coming after us, I'm sure of it."

"So? By the time they catch us, we'll be in the new world, and we'll have cover and resources at our disposal that they just won't have. Our head start is our advantage, so come down from there and for the love of god, get a tan. You don't want your victory portrait to showcase a pale conqueror for history to remember you by."

"I'm going to stay right here. If you want to bring the book to me over here, and re-hang the hammock so be it. But I'm not going to give up watch."

"We have two people doing just that from the crow's nest."

"Those jerks? They couldn't keep watch on a fly."

"I don't understand..."

"Forget it. If you're not going to bring me my book, then just go away. I'm fine right here, without your help."

"Sir, don't get snippy."

"Snippy? I'll get however I want! Snippy? I'll show you snippy when I cut off your..."

"Now let's not get violent, sir, remember what your therapist told you. Deep breaths, thankfulness. Maybe stretch a little."

"If she was a good therapist, she'd have come along. I'm stuck with you now."

"If you're going to be rude, maybe I will leave you alone to wallow."

"Wallow. Bah. I don't care what you say. No one's going to remember you anyway, so why should I pay you any mind?"

"Again. Rude. Bye." The navigator walked away, and Cortes turned back to scour the sea for ships on the horizon.

"Only 100 more miles... with this crappy wind, just a few more days till landfall..." Cortes took a deep breath. "Should have got a faster ship."

*****

The Chief walked into the throne room to find the Vizier sitting at a table with dozens of tablets strewn about with his hammer and chisel at the ready.

"Hey buddy, how's it coming? Heard back from anyone yet?"

"Your Majesty! Umm not yet. It's been a couple days, so hopefully we'll know anytime. For the sake of the elotes," he chuckled uneasily.

"What's wrong, Vizier? You don't look rested."

"I'm rested! Don't worry about me; I'm just finishing up some invoices. I'll be speaking to the mariachis this afternoon."

"Did you get the same guys from my birthday?"

"Yeah, they were available. They asked for a song list, do you have any requests or should I just tell them to figure something out?"

"Mmmm, just tell them nothing that would be a downer... or anything thoughtful. This is going to be a fun party, carefree, and so on. I don't want this to turn into a Damien Rice concert."

The Vizier chiseled, as he spoke aloud, "No Damien. Rice."

"Perfect. I'll be in the tub. By the way, where is my slave? My neck has been sweating like crazy, and it just occurred to me that I haven't had my blood treatment in several days."

"I have him running errands for the party."

"Ohh. Okay. Next time tell me first though. Find me an interim slave." He exited to his personal quarters.

"Interim slave. Great. An assistant for me would be awesome too, but is there ever anything budgeted for me? No, of course not. 'Would you like overtime, Vizier?' 'Why, yes that would be lovely! Also blood my neck, it's rather hot.' 'Of course, Vizier, you must be so hot because you're so important.' 'Thanks for that, assistant! Now blood me! Chop chop!' "

The Chief peaked his head out from behind his curtain. "Vizier, stop talking to yourself, this is why people cross the street when they see you." The Vizier's face contorted. "I'll show them... I should've listened to my mother, politics are no place to be..."

"Vizier! What did I say?"

The Vizier shut up at last. "Thank you! Kukulkan on a cracker!"

*****

The P.O.W entered the town of the Nahuas that afternoon and was immediately greeted by the guards standing watch by forest's edge.

"Holy crap! Cacique Jr., is that you??" The P.O.W dropped his bag of invites, which shattered on the ground, and smiled.

"It is I! So good to see you, friends!"

"How did you escape? Was there an epic battle? Did you slay the Chief?" asked the younger guard.

"Haha no, nothing like that. You're never going to believe what happened. Come, let's find our Chief and I'll tell everyone the story together."

The three of them skipped into town, through grassy patches and between pueblos, till they arrived at the less opulent but still pretty nice mansion of the Nahua Chief. Now I know what you're thinking... if Cacique Jr. was so high in stature that he could waltz into the palace, and by extension must logically be a nobleman, then why did the Nahuas leave him to rot in the Mayan Chief's palace? Well, the answer is simple! He wasn't noble at all, but a Nahua slave! They just happened to be much nicer to their property there.

The Nahua Chief greeted him with a hug and asked him about his travels, and he explained, as he was a natural storyteller, that the Mayan advisor convinced the Chief to throw another festival for the Pale Lispy Seafarers of lore. His tale brought tears of laughter to the faces of the Nahua council. "What kind of idiot would do that again? Fooleth me once..."

"That's exactly the logic they took in trusting the Vizier! Saying that if they were fooled last time, then the second time, the prophecy must be true," Cacique Jr. laughed. "So I was sent to invite the Nahua people to the great party for the Lispy ones."

"Yeah, not gonna happen. It was too much of a strain on the economy last time to put the people through another journey through the forests for nothing. Especially since this is an election year."

"Well consider yourself invited."

"Thank you, Cacique Jr., you may retake your post. I'm a bit warm, would you get the blood cup for me?"

*****

"Hernan! So great to see you down here! Have you finally taken solace in the fact that the Cubans aren't coming?" The Navigator poured Cortes a glass of wine and plopped it on the table in front of him. The galley was full of jovial Spaniards, eating and drinking to their hearts' content. The chef also happened to be a rather talented flamenco guitarist and was strumming away like his life depended on it.

"I think so, but I was getting hungry. And I heard music. So I figured I'd give it a rest." He sat down at the officers' table and grabbed a bread roll. "What have you all been up to?"

The Navigator spoke up, "Well with my estimates, we should land on water's edge in two more dawns and one more dusk. We seem to be on track by the stars. That's about it really."

Cortes looked around the table. The other officers nodded in agreement. "Yeah, not much to do on a boat," admitted the general.

"Well... sounds good boys. Two more dawns and we'll be off this blasted floating hovel. Pass the butter?"

*****

The Vizier paced around Town Square. The blood fountain was built, and the plumber got the blood to cascade, so that was good. The traveling zoo was set up. Exotic creatures of all shapes and sizes growled from their cages, filling the square with sounds of the jungle. But there was still no word from the Nahuas or the Aztecs. *Jerks, don't even have the decency to let us know they're not coming. Last time I invite those chumps to anything. More lispy friends for us.* About twenty-four more hours remained until they arrived. The Chief was breathing down his neck hard now, but worse still, the elotes woman—a great grandmother herself, mind you—was even more aggressive than the Chief.

"How many attendees, Vizier? I need a headcount three days ago."

"I don't know exactly! The out-of-towners still haven't gotten their confirmed numbers to me."

"Well you better take a guess, because I won't have the food ready in time, and it'll be you, not me that looks dumb. It says on the sign outside my pueblo, *must provide accurate headcount for catered events at least 48 hours in advance.* I'm covered if this is another big failure, and you'll be scooping shit on the roadside when this house of cards tumbles."

"God! Just make it four hundred," he snapped.

"Four hundred? So the Nahuas and the Aztec are coming?"

"Who the hell knows, just make them please. I don't have time anymore to be conservative about this."

"Okay, it's your funeral."

"If you keep up that tone, it'll be yours."

"Not bloody likely, I'm still the highest rated elotes vendor in town, the Chief would never allow it."

"The Chief will have to deal with it, because I'm twelve seconds away from strangling you."

"With those hands? Hah!" The elotes woman laughed as she reentered her shop, and closed the door right in his face. The Vizier growled to himself as he stormed off. At least his checklist was taken care of. All would be ready, and Kukulkan willing, there'd be guests, however disrespectful they were for not RSVPing.

*****

"LAND HO!" shouted the lookout from his perch. The crew fell over themselves climbing out of bed to take a look at their new homeland. Sure enough, in the distance, a beach covered in trees and vegetation lurked within reach. Cortes pulled out his pocket telescope and looked toward the beach. A small robed man was waving wildly at the ship.

"Oyy! General, come look at this!" Cortes handed his telescope to the general, and the two exchanged surprised glances. "I wonder what that's about."

The ships (by the way, there were twelve of them—Cortes wasn't known for being coy) dropped anchor and landing boats were lowered into the surf. Cortes was the first to jump out of his lander and walked up to the robed man. The man was balding up top, and had a surprisingly large belly for one that appeared to be trapped on this island.

"Hello there," began Cortes, extending his hand for a hearty shake.

"Good morning! Beautiful day, no?" asked the stranger with a smile.

"Quite. My name is Hernan Cortes, leader of the Cuban task force to set up a colony here in the name of Mother España. What's your name?

"Hello Señor Cortes, pleasure to make your acquaintance. My name is Geronimo de Aguilar. I'm a Franciscan who's had the misfortune of unfair seas. Wonderful to see Spanish faces after so long."

"How long have you been here?" questioned Cortes.

"God knows. You're here to build a colony?"

"Yep, I'm rather eager to fortify our crew, we may or may not have been followed, and it would be ideal to hold the higher ground should that happen."

"Great! Sounds awesome to me, man. Now there's a small wrinkle: on the coast here, there aren't any resources of value, they get washed away with the weather from time to time. The good stuff's all on the island interior, protected by the Maya. But good news, they're pretty nice when you get to know them, and the Chief is actually super eager to meet you."

"Me? How does he know about me?"

"He said there's some prophecy, blah blah blah, anyways, who cares. The point is, I bet if we come as a team, we can make a good impression and co-habitate without much trouble."

"Perfect," said Cortes, "I'm not looking to rock the boat, we'd love to meet these Maya you speak of, and if we can all be friends, all the better. I'd rather not have a blunder on my hands like that Columbus dummy, and get Spaniards hurt unnecessarily."

"Shall we?" asked Geronimo.

"Indeed! General, Navigator, you're coming with me. We'll ride with our new friend here to visit the Chief. Tell the slaves to dig rocks from the beach and begin building fortifications in the event that the Cubans do come."

"Yessir!" The General retreated to inform the men.

"Where did you get that robe, by the way? I like the cut of it."

"I made it myself, actually! From monkey hair.

"Get outta town, it looks really comfortable." Cortes climbed aboard his steed and kicked it in the ribs. The men rode inward.

*****

The Vizier bounced a ball he made against a wall in the throne room. He had grown irritable and restless with no good news coming his way from the neighboring tribes. The door to the chamber burst open, and a lowly lookout from the far side of town came running in.

"Chief! Chief!!" he panted. The Chief emerged from his bedroom.

"Yes?" he asked casually.

"The Pale Seafarers are near! Their water horses have stopped offshore, and the men entered the forest! They are coming! They are coming!"

"Then there's no time to lose! Alert the town to get into their places, light the torches, instruct the mariachis, and begin the festival! I want it to seem like the party has already begun, so we don't look too eager!"

"Yes, Your Majesty!" The lookout ran from their presence dutifully.

"Vizier, everything's ready right?"

"Yes!... almost," he trailed off.

"Sorry what was that? Did you say, 'almost'?"

"Well, yeah, everything's pretty much ready."

"What does that mean, pretty much?

"It means, *mostly.*"

"What still needs to be done? Our foreign visitors are upon us! Did the zoo arrive?"

"Yes, yes, the zoo's here, the fountain's done, the food is good."

"You pulled off the fountain? Was it reasonable?"

"Yeah, not as bad as you'd think," he said with pride.

"Well done! But then if the blood fountain is erected and the monkeys are in place, what is left?"

"Okay, so I don't think the Nahuas or the Aztecs are coming."

"Why not?" the Chief was suddenly cranky. "They didn't even have to set up or clean up, they just needed to come and have fun!"

"That's what I said! But no, they never RSVP'd and the wood scouts said there was no trace of them within our borders. I think they blew us off."

"Those jerks! What the hell!? You know what, forget them then; we don't need them. Make a note: do not invite the Nahuas or the Aztecs to my next birthday. I don't care if they had fun last time, they're not welcome anymore."

"Done, sir."

"Well what's left for us, right now?"

"Just to be ready for the arrival of the lispy ones."

"Let's get down there then." The Chief wrapped his arm around the Vizier and prompted him to stroll at his side. "I know you've been killing yourself for this party, and though I may have been sassy from time to time, I'm proud of your work here. You did good. And when I'm re-elected, you're getting a raise. And an assistant." The Chief winked at the Vizier and they walked to the party.

*****

"Here we are, Señor Cortes! Just through here." The men rode over the last tiny stream and through a layer of trees into a clearing. "Surprise!!!!" the Maya shouted to Cortes and his crew. The Maya applauded and the Chief approached the obviously shocked Cortes and Geronimo, and shook their hands.

"Welcome my friends, you have entered the kingdom of the Maya. We have been so anxious to meet you for as long as I can remember! How was your journey?"

A little overwhelmed, Cortes regained his composure amid the sea of foreign faces. "It was okay, not too bad. The weather was with us, thankfully, though the wind was dead for a lot of the time."

"Sorry to hear it! Well, if you'll follow me, we have so many things planned." The Chief guided the Spaniards into their town square, when a roar erupted across the air.

"Jesus Christ, what was that!?" panicked Hernan.

"Oh don't worry, pale man, that is the traveling zoo we brought in for your arrival! I think you'll be most pleased with it. In fact, as a special treat, the zookeeper informed me that we have the last gaggle of Chupacabra in existence for your viewing pleasure. I'll show you soon, first let us eat and drink as I'm certain you're tired from your journey."

"Thank you, we are a little tired."

"Right this way!" The Chief sat them down at a long table covered in a cornucopia of foods usually reserved only for hosting local warlords.

The Spaniards dug right in, alongside the Maya. They ate and drank till the sun set, while the music coated the air in a buttery goodness that allowed everyone to let their collective hair down.

"What wonderful hosts you are!" exclaimed Hernan.

"Why thank you, pale man! You honor us with your presence." The Chief smiled across the table.

"Cortes, my name is Hernan Cortes."

"Pleasure to meet you Hernan Cortes. Are you and your men comfortable?"

"Yes, quite, I reckon, thank you," he said politely.

"Good, I'm glad. Allow me to show you some of our animals."

The men stood up. Cortes grabbed his belly.

"Is everything okay, Hernan Cortes?" asked the Chief with some concern.

"Oh yes, friend, it's just... food baby!" he rubbed his stomach, and the men laughed.

"Right this way!"

They strolled into the zoo, and the Chief proudly showed the Spaniard various large cats, including panthers, leopards, and puma, as well as their collection of varying apes and exotic birds.

"Allow me to show you our pride and joy, Hernan Cortes, right over here." They walked up to a smaller cage, and Cortes squatted down to see the creatures inside.

"What are they called, friend?"

"These my pale brother, are the last five Chupacabra alive. We freed them from the distant Aztec Zoo after a local whistleblower told everyone how they were being treated. The zoo is now being investigated."

The smallest Chupacabra, just a pup really, walked up to the bars of the cage and growled.

"Oh so cute! What's the little guy's name?" asked Hernan.

"That one is my favorite too, it's actually a girl. I named it after my old slave girl, "Malinalli." But the wife wasn't keen on her so we sent the girl back to her Nahua family, so this is my last connection to her. My little Malinche."

"What a lovely name! Hola Malinche... ahhhchooo!"

Hernan sneezed violently, startling the little creature that ran back to its mama.

"Excuse me. So sorry!" Hernan was mortified.

"Oh, that's quite alright, they're sturdy little beasts. Are you cold?" inquired the Chief.

"I am, rather."

"Tonight is a little strange, it's been so warm for a week leading up to this. There must be a storm coming, for tonight is extra chilly, I can feel it. Allow me to send for some cloaks to warm us."

"No, good Chief, you've been so kind to us already, and I'm sure our fast friendship will endure for ages to come. Allow me to extend the courtesy to you and yours."

"That's most generous of you, Hernan Cortes."

"It's nothing, please, it would be my pleasure."

"Well thank you, friend."

Hernan called for his servant, and the Chief leaned over to the Vizier and whispered, "This is going so well, don't you think?"

The Vizier gave him a hearty thumbs up and smiled. The Spanish servant ran over in a hurry.

"Yes, commander?" asked the trusty servant.

"Run to the ship, in the storage room below deck next to the infirmary are our stockpile of blankets. Bring them here and make sure every single Maya is given one, to thank them for their hospitality," commanded Cortes.

"Yessir!" The boy departed promptly into the woods.

Hernan smiled at his hosts, next to the few endangered Chupacabra. "Yes, my friends, tonight is the start of a beautiful friendship!"

"Posthumous Remarks From a Live Man"

January, 1864 — Gettysburg, Pennsylvania, United States

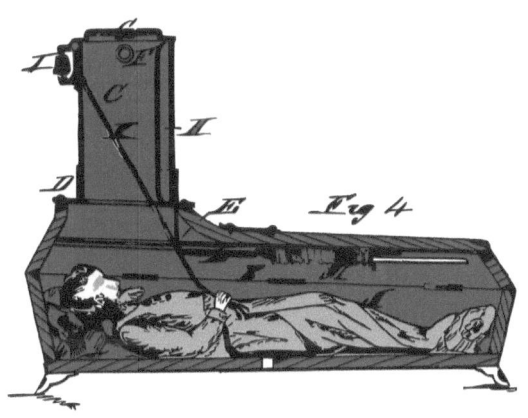

"It's a rare psychological condition known as Hypochondria. And in the case of your husband, I'm afraid it could prove terminal, Mrs. Henries." The physician put his hand on my shoulder to console me, but I felt rather more dumbstruck than distraught.

"What the devil do you mean terminal?"

"Well... it's an interesting case. I've seen the condition only a few times, usually deriving in patients under more stressful circumstances. Perhaps soldiers or politicians for instance. But that's why this is so unique, since he is obviously facing different hurdles."

"Hurdles. The man couldn't jump a hurdle if he was a horse." I sighed, looking through the window at the shell of a man I married so long ago. He looked back at me like a baby. Full of dumb curiosity, but no real understanding of what was befalling him.

"I meant that in the figurative sense."

"Doctor, please explain to me how he can suffer from terminal Hypochondria."

"Normally, as you seem familiar with the ailment, one just gets to worrying. Maybe they saw someone in town with a sickness, then they think they have it. 'I have a cough, I must have black lung,' that sort of thing. But your husband, for some unknown reason, seems to be actually developing debilitating external symptoms from his internal paranoia. I've run all tests available. I've listened to his vitals, examined his eyes and throat. Checked his temperature. His urine sample appears normal. He seems to think he has Cholera. He is pale. His throat and eyes are dry. He says he has abdominal cramps—but that could just be gas. Furthermore, he has mostly windy diarrhea versus conventional, and vomiting only occurs right after he eats the hospital food—but that could also be a coincidence. You've said he's been in and out of hospital for awhile?"

"Indeed. Right about a decade."

"My word."

"Yes. I think he has taken a bit of guilt to heart. Of what, I dare not say, for it is his transgression, but that was right about the time it all began."

"Poor man." The physician breathed onto his spectacles and wiped off the steam with a handkerchief.

"Poor indeed. What is next to be done?"

"Alas, I've never seen a perfectly well person exhibit so much Cholera. He hasn't been drinking much. His eyes are beginning to sink in."

"Yes, but what is left to be done?"

"I suppose call a minister. Give his soul some peace. And hope he starts drinking his water soon."

"A minister. So he's actually near the end then?"

"I am so sorry for you and your family. If you need anything from me, don't hesitate to ask."

The doctor tipped his hat, and left me alone in the hallway. I could not speak for a time, but I weighed my options in my mind. My husband tried to focus on me through the window in his room, to gauge my expressions I'd surmise, but quickly began to tire and passed out instead. Which was all well and good. *No news is good news, wretched husband.*

*****

I closed my eyes for a few moments, but a clanking noise down the hallway wrenched me out of my nap. When I opened my eyes, I was once again surrounded by my family.

My name is Henry by the way. How rude of me not to start with introductions. I shall now explain to you the why and the wherefore for the exchange I had just witnessed between my Beloved and my physician.

It was winter in Gettysburg. The clime was bleak, as you could imagine. Perhaps Mother Nature could sense the unrest that our nation was enduring. Perhaps she was dying... like me. While the battle there was long over, bloodstained heaps of earth littered the grounds. Some of the children from the hospital, upon consent given by their physician, would actually go out and play in the snow. Nothing is as horrendous as bloody Snowmen. Especially if you put a Union uniform on them—that would hit too close to home. Fortunately most of the kids built bloody Snowkids—it's much easier to stomach, as they resemble workers on any Tuesday in one of the nearby factories. Now I was no warrior myself, but the terrifying memories of Gettysburg, or as the locals called them, "Getty Images," created an aura of death all through town. Though I was certain I was being haunted even before the battle.

At this point, I was holed up in a former Confederate military hospital for about a week with some strange ailment. My breathing had grown faint in recent days. As I stared up at the same shriveled ceiling joist with a pathetic cobweb barely holding on, the dying spider crawled into its corner for the last time and laid its feeble head there. I tried to loosen my collar with my hand, but I could barely lift my arms. My previously undiagnosed condition was, for days, growing worse every morn, stabilizing before noon, and by nightfalls the nurses repeatedly warned my loyal family that my time could be nearing... before I'd come to again in the morning and the process would begin anew. But this morning was different. This morning the doctor knew what was upon me.

My family would sit by my feet crying faintly or knitting to pass the time. My grandsons, Nathaniel and Tobias, ten and twelve respectively, would play on the floor with wooden horses or makeshift spears crafted from broken pencils, completely unawares or at least completely without care that they sat adjacent to a breathing corpse. My steadfast wife, Nancy, a stunning woman of thirty-five years of age, with the eyes of a hawk and the radiant hair of a Cherub, held my toes atop the thin blanket from her rocker, trying never to look at me because of the pain it caused her to see me in this state. My sons, all grown now, would come and go from their shops in the town with an air of apathy, for once I died they would not inherit much, save for my copper spittoon or my old rusted plow collecting dust behind my shed. They were businessmen each, and had little time for an ailing old fool, even if that fool was their father.

For days, with every inhalation I could feel less air saturate my blood, and I'd grow more tired, suffocating in my own skin. The worst of it all, Nancy explained upon my awakening this day, was that I was afflicted with some French-sounding disorder known as *Hippocamembert*. Nothing I had heard of. Nothing representative of my symptoms. Nothing they could cure. I'd soon fade away like the elderly sod I always was and would be till no mortal would remember my name. A few times I'd cry too, but my lethargy would overtake me and I'd just fall asleep instead, awakening in a state of confusion and disorientation to the gentle rub of my toe by my faithful Beloved.

On the third day in hospice I was sure this would be my last one alive, and I was afraid for what lie beyond. No one could mistake me for a saint, or seldom even a sinner. But, and I say this with some reluctance, that I had failed my vows as a husband and laid with another some ten years before. The young woman's gorgeous glow was enough to render me helpless and we made our way to the barn behind my family's home where I sinned before God and wife, who would discover us that very afternoon. I was ashamed, as my bride never strayed nor seemed compelled to, but after that day the twinkle in her eye never returned and I knew that the Eden I was allowed entrance to was taken from me by my own wicked design and I would be granted paradise nevermore.

She stayed by my side thereafter, and we never spoke of it, but our love was tainted like the waters of a backwater well, and she was alone despite my daily presence. I had brought shame on our home and she couldn't speak of it to her sisters or anyone without fear of exile from polite society. Like I now, she was trapped in her place without hope for tomorrow, and I loathed myself daily for it.

And yet, all said and done, I feared every breath I managed this day, for my remaining cycles of respiration could be counted in three digits. I would die before sundown, and I'd never be able to make my wife happy again and she'd be left with this decrepit husk in her memory in the sunset of our lives. She was too mature to bear further children—no man would have her henceforth, and she'd be alone till she joined me in eternal peril where I'd feel her sadness look upon me once more and forever. Unless you believed

Dante: then I'd be blown around in the wind getting motion sickness forever while my scorned wife danced on clouds. I don't rather think that's my destiny—I've heard the stories: If I'm not chewing on brimstone candy for my eternity, I'll eat my hat!

When the high bells of noon struck, a chaplain entered my room and mirrored my Beloved at the opposite corner of my deathbed. He pulled from his shirt pocket a humble hardbound black leather bible with golden trim. He cleared his throat and replaced his spectacles on his nose to read my Last Rites and await the end with my family surrounding us.

His quivering voice began, but faded to the background of my consciousness as my mind wandered to days of my youth when I'd play in the brook and capture small feral dogs to domesticate for my own pleasure. I considered my best friends, Bucky and Chester, and our chunky friend we called Walnut, and all the fun we'd had exploring the gold mine at the corner of town. They all, now dead in battle, seemed to enter the room as ghosts to witness my passing. This war that slain Bucky, Chester, and Walnut, that had touched every aspect of American life, now seemed destined to end the American existence as we knew it. Perhaps my dying was better now, as I don't know if I could bear the End of Days. Regardless, fear gripped my heart ever stronger and my chest tightened and I couldn't catch my breath. The chaplain kindly pressed his palm upon my sternum and spoke his holy words directly to me so I could hear every syllable and I was assuaged for the time.

As his personal sermon neared its end, a loud bang was heard from down the hallway, and shortly another as well. A few seconds later the door to our room was hurled open with a loud impertinence and a man scruffy in dress and disheveled in nature looked around impatiently for the chaplain.

He placed his hand on the holy man's back and led him to the far corner of the room where he whispered some unknown monologue. As he spoke, my grandsons and my wife left my side and huddled up with the men. The stranger started again, careful to keep his voice at a level below my hearing.

With his message delivered, there was a silence while his words sank in, and he bowed to me, tipped his hat, and took his leave. Following his departure, Nancy and my grandsons whispered back and forth, and the chaplain interjected, but all out of earshot until a point came where they had come to some kind of an accord. My family and the chaplain re-took their positions at my bedside, but the gears were cranking in their minds and a strange energy befell the room. I was too weak to ask what was said, but it seemed a scheme was in the works, for not long later Nathanial came to my side and gently sat me up, while Tobias entered from the hallway dragging a wheelchair to my side.

The boys lifted me from my bed into the chair and I was at a loss. The chaplain removed his belt and wrapped it around the chair to restrain me from flopping on the floor like a marionette. Whilst my eldest grandson pushed, my wife, walking parallel, held my head up so I could see where we tread, and I noticed the family was parading down the hallway towards the reception desk of the hospital. But they showed no signs of slowing, and Nathaniel opened the entrance with a burst of white light that I hadn't seen in I couldn't remember how long. Probably just a few days, but it felt like an eon. My eyes burned and I tried to look away, but still my Love held me firm and we were outside.

A compact horse-drawn carriage stood by out front, and my grandsons and wife lifted me from the chair into the carriage where I was once again tied in with the chaplain's belt. My family, as well as the chaplain himself, walked off into the snow-covered grass beyond the hospital, and I was alone with the balding carriage driver, who turned to ensure I was locked in tight. He wore a crisp black suit, but traces of dust or dirt littered small areas of the garment and likewise patches of dust dotted his face. He turned to his horses and bid them march and the carriage was off before I could utter a word to protest.

*****

"I don't quite understand, Grandmama." Nathanial told me as we walked along through the snow bank beside the road.

"What would you like to know, my little dear?" I asked the boy whose knowledge on matters of medicine extended to, 'Say ahh!'"

"Why are we going there?"

"Yes, Grandmama, why there?" The two tikes turned on me. "It's not a sterile environment, after all," Tobias reasoned.

"It is. In a way." I considered my statement. Perhaps a little dark, admittedly. But as they say, *desperate times.* "All will be clear, my darlings. Fear not. Your Grandmama understands, and that's enough for now. So be good little ones, and help Grandmama today. This is not your every day." To lighten the mood, I picked up a ball of snow and hurled it at Tobias, smacking him in the shirt.

"Oh shoot. Come here boy, I've bloodied you."

*****

The ride was uncomfortable and the cart bounced frequently over holes in the road and rocks in the way. The belt dutifully restrained me, but I was sure I'd pop out and die in an undignified heap under the horses' feet. This was all too strange a trip for one on the cusp of the beyond.

After a time we came to a clearing, and as the sun was setting behind a line of high trees, I saw them: my wife and grandsons, the chaplain, and the strange man from my room. Call it adrenaline or what have you, but I mustered the energy to eke out a few words. "Who... Who is... that man... Who is he?... Where are we going?"

"Shush man, your time is nearing."

"My time?" I echoed.

"I said shush!" The driver placed his fingers over my lips and pulled back on the reins, and the horses came to a stop. He untied the belt and lifted me carefully from the carriage into an awaiting wheel chair. And it was then that I saw it: beyond the cart and next to my wife, already dressed in mourning attire, was a cold mound of dirt and a hole awaiting its meal. Me.

I was too weak to resist, and the driver now pushed me in my wheel chair over the hilly terrain and dark grassy earth to grave's edge. The chaplain resumed his Last Rites and crossed me with holy water, unawares of my tremendous sin some years back. It was a worse sin to not confess and be buried in hallowed ground, and it was obvious what would befall me now: my fate was a living burial without confession! I could feel the silent rage of the archangel's gaze upon my visage, and a holy man himself would unknowingly deprive my right to make peace with my Creator. My being was torn asunder and I could feel my heart pumping like none I'd felt before.

I tried to speak, to confess, to everything I had done, and wipe clean the dirty slate that was my wife's betrayed heart, but I was gagged, and the driver made sure I couldn't say another word. My young grandsons hopped into the grave below and there I saw a wooden coffin, unremarkable in every way except that this one would be my resting place. Not even a satin pillow to rest my head on like dignified carrion. I was one layer removed from a vulture's midnight snack.

The driver and my wife removed me from the chair and I dangled like a newborn babe above the frigid ground, and once again I saw the man that forced entry into my room and persuaded my family to turn against me like a common criminal at the executioner's block. He picked his tooth with a stick and rested his foot atop my tombstone, already in place at the head of the grave, where I saw my name written in shoddy bold letters and a phrase I couldn't stand to read: "Here lies Henry Henries, Born 1819, Forgotten 1864."

My grandsons grabbed my feet and I was lowered into the grave where I felt all these hands upon my body, and my mind ran askew as I saw the children's innocent faces turn red and horns grow from their little demonic heads, laughing as they pressed me into this coffin like a chambermaid putting away spare linens in a storage box under a bed. I looked around in terror, and their little angelic faces returned to normal, and I was sure I had gone mad. My gag was removed forcefully and the boys climbed from the pit of despair, while the interloper and driver descended to take their place.

When I was tucked in, the last thing I saw as the lid closed over the top of me was a grand brass bell next to the tombstone with a string dangling down into my eternal resting hole. The lid placed in position, the chaplain shouted so I could hear, "May everlasting God take pity upon your eternal soul, and may you rest in peaceful slumber till Christ comes again on the last day in vengeful judgment of all Creation!"

Then on cue, random thuds overhead fell atop the coffin, and I knew it was true: they were filling the hole with dirt and I would never look upon my devoted wife again. The thuds slowly intensified as I wept in my box, before they got softer and softer, and I knew the dirt was thick enough overhead that I was done. My chest ached with sorrow and I gasped for air in that unholy casket, urging myself to scream and kick and punch the shabby hold above me. I shrieked like a maiden in a dark alleyway, and pounded, and then I remembered the brass bell above ground! *A Safety Coffin! There might be hope yet!*

I maneuvered and contorted my body, as much as I could bear, to grab the silk rope behind my head, and with all my might I tugged on the rope again and again, over and over, though I couldn't hear it none. I sobbed and tugged the rope and wheezed, cursing my infidelity, cursing my weakness, cursing my spendthrift habits leaving my children and grandchildren with nothing but regret that they ever knew me.

I screamed in my box, "Dear God! Please forgive me my sins and weaknesses, I am a flawed pile of meat that doesn't deserve your providence, yet I wish I could undo my failings to preserve the dignity of my spouse and my young, for they deserve your love and your grace! Please Lord of all, please forgive me, and grant them peace, though I deserve none! For you are the architect of all, and I'm not worthy to shine your boots, but take pity on *her*, for she is your sacred child and I have wronged her!"

I shouted for what felt like an hour, though it was likely less time, and pulled on that bell intensely, hoping some passerby would hear it and take pity. But as I screamed I grew light headed as the air had grown thin, and I rang only thrice more before I finally fainted.

I don't know how long I was inside the damned box, but my head was splitting when I came to, my vision a blur, and my lungs sore from shouting. There I saw my family adjacent my bed in the hospital, and the chaplain too, looking at me smiling. *It was all some ghastly dream!* "It was all a dream!" I mouthed at first, and repeated over again louder and stronger several times. "It was all a terrible dream!" The doctors entered and pulled scopes and devices to check my anatomy while I repeated those words.

"Dear wife, you are my shining star and I am blessed to look upon you once more! I have wronged you and I have sinned! I am a stain on our family crest! Father, I wish to engage in confession before it is too late!" The priest smiled, while the doctors examined me. He said nothing at first, just watched the physicians.

"It is astonishing! I've never seen anything like this! His vitals are up, his respiration improving with each moment. He's energetic and speaking and his heart rate is fine! What a miracle! Though he may have soiled himself. We'll have to keep an eye on that," proclaimed the lead physician, replacing his scope around his neck.

The chaplain turned his attention back to me. "My son, you are wiped clean. I heard your confessions through the bell shaft, you are eligible to enter heaven... once it is your time."

"What do you mean?" I looked around at my family for some explanation, and as I scanned the group, my gaze fell upon the man from my tombstone eating an apple with a smug little grin. I now noticed a Confederate medal affixed to his overcoat. He was one of them, come back for revenge!

"It's you!" I recoiled in terror, and my sons, now in attendance, restrained me.

"It is I. But fear not Mr. Henries. You are cured!"

"Cured? Cured of what? Hippocamembert?"

"Cured of *death*, Henries."

"I'm sorry, but I do not take your meaning, you crude interloper."

The physician returned to my side, and tried to calm me a little.

"Henry, this man here came at my behest. He has been conducting experimental treatments for some of our more... tenuous ailments."

The man interjected, "You *knew* you would die, did you not, Mr. Henries?"

I considered his words for a moment. "Surely, but what of it?"

"The mind is a powerful machine, sir—if you accept you will die, you will die. So I gave you a funeral. Before your time had come. So you realized you should not die because of your untimely burial, and so it is! You are cured! We overcame death with the specter of it. And now you are cured."

"I've never heard of such a thing!" I shouted at him confused and angry that he tormented me so. He took a bite of his apple and through fruit filled teeth rebutted, "Well now you have." He put his cap back on his head and with that he bowed to my wife and my sons, to the chaplain and doctors, and took his leave. *The scoundrel!*

My sons smiled to each other and bid my wife farewell, taking my grandsons with them. The chaplain too, departed and the doctors resumed their duties. The room was now silent and peaceful again, and my wife pulled her rocking chair up to my side and took my hand, staring directly into my eyes.

"My Dear, I am..." I began.

"Shush, my husband, I know. With body mended and soul wiped clean, you and I too can begin the healing. But tell me once more, just so I can hear it from your lips to my ears."

"I love you as deep and sacredly as my own grave. And with all my soul I will become worthy of you once again."

She kissed my hand in hers. A look in her eyes seemed suddenly unsettled, but she quickly stood and walked to the door to watch the hospital staff resume their business as usual. She sighed, presumably of relief, and took her place next to me.

"Dearest one. You understand life has been very difficult these ten years?"

"It pains me that it pains you so!"

"Why would you have strayed to begin with? Was I not desirable?" she asked calmly, resigned.

"You were always desirable. And are still. I don't know what compelled me that cruel day, but I know I've suffered daily because of my failing."

"The doctor tells me you will make a full recovery. You may live another fifteen, twenty years."

"A miracle!" I shouted and clasped my hands together in praise. My wife once again stood and walked to the windows in the room and closed the curtains so the light would not hurt my eyes, before taking her place at my side again. She sat for a moment in silence, contemplating something.

"Did you know the bed you lie in now was utilized by none other than General Lee over the summer?" she mustered at last.

"This old feather bag? By the devil himself? I was not aware he had come to hospital."

"It was a quick trip, I'm told. Sprained pinky or some such."

"Too bad it wasn't a sprained heart! I would that he died in this bed, so that our union may prevail! But what does it matter? If the world ends tomorrow, at least I have you till the end," I said with all my heart.

"Shall I fluff your pillow, Beloved?" Nancy said, looking past me to the corner of the room, almost in a trance.

"You are an angel most holy," I replied lifting my head for her to extract it. She took the cushion between her hands and gave it a whack or two, aligning the feathers into a fresh configuration. She smiled at me, and ran her fingers through my hair, and I closed my eyes, for the gentle caress of her fingers in my scalp was rejuvenating and I felt like a babe with its mother for the first time.

*****

I kissed him on the forehead. But it did not provide me the sweetness I had hoped for when first the scruffy man promised a cure. I could tell my husband felt like a kitten in my arms. And yet, something had changed. Something of his rebirth and renewal pinged like a sour note in my heart's chambers. I knew now everything was different. It could not revert back again. I said to him in a gentle voice, "You have been given a second chance that no one else gets. I'm glad you are reprieved."

He smiled again and cuddled my arm. I balanced his pillow on my hip while he nestled down into his well-worn hospital bunk. "I love you," I said, perhaps trying to reassure myself.

"I love you." He echoed back.

"I really do," I said. I let the words rest on the air until they fell like feathers on the floor. "But, a slate so clean is best stored above the mantel. Like an urn. No reason to tarnish it."

He settled onto his back and looked at me without any understanding in the world. I considered his words, *"If the world ends tomorrow, at least I have you till the end."*

"Be well in heaven, my Sweet." *The end is such a tentative concept.*

*****

60

She replaced the pillow over my face and pushed down firmly until I became lightheaded and faint and went limp. Then she pushed down a bit longer. When finally she had decided I was dead enough, she tossed the pillow to the side and straightened out my hair. She kissed me again on the lips. This time her eyes had the warm glow I remember from before. She whispered into the room, "Tomorrow is not the end. Tomorrow is a new day. Sweet dreams."

Maybe we should have just gotten divorced.

"The Ways To Make Gemütlichkeit, or: Foodie and the Beast"

Early Autumn, 1978 — Liechtenstein

Once long ago, on a faraway hill, in the grand countryside up a deep dark path in the country of Liechtenstein, stood the house of a man named Herr Vongrüber Gemütlichkeit. Vongrüber was a former Gefreiter in the German army back when he was a young man, and fought in the Great War... of the Damned. It was called such because in those early days a terrible plague rose up to rival those of Haitian horror stories told round the campfire, in which Voodoo Kings possessed the average man's body and mind with a dark and ominous force.

Vongrüber had been witness to these damned folks firsthand when he was a boy, even before he joined the fight against them. His sister, who was playing in the yard of their humble German split-level, was attacked and lost her thumbs when they were both eaten off by a pair of the terrible creatures. She had been given the cure in time and was sufficiently neurotic for the rest of her days, but Vongrüber was not a man who quickly forgot or forgave. For example, when he was a boy of five, he got bumped in line at The Majestic Mouse theme park waiting for the bathroom. Forty years later, that now-old man that long ago bumped Vongrüber found himself being bumped back... out the window of a third story bathroom by a beaming middle-aged hobbyist named Gemütlichkeit.

The Dead gave rise to Vongrüber's desire to protect himself. He trained in the army, and they taught him how to run and how to fire a gun. They taught him knife skills, knot techniques, and how to cook delicious frozen meals over a campfire with just a spoon and some Himalayan salt. Step one: *complete.* He was not an awkward dork who wet himself every time he saw the damned. Several times, he even covered his shirtless body in mud and attacked herds of the creatures himself, with only his tacky red muslin bandana as protection.

His smug attitude toward them led him to the next step: *use psychological warfare by running a brutal campaign of decapitations and slaughter to put a hearty fear into them.* This plan did not really work as they had no neurons firing upstairs, and thus were incapable of fear, in the same way that you could not take a pet dog and seduce it with some deep bass and scented candles.

Since the nation's handsomest pharmaceutical scientists had already established the cure, the general population did not really have much need to destroy them anymore. They discovered that a concentrated dose of the aerosol dropped from a plane over a city would alleviate the woes of the recently bitten victims, and just allow the decaying masses to keel over. The "damned" disease was going away. There were barely enough cases left to make the matter worth a second glance.

In recent months, Vongrüber went looking for a new place to live and stumbled onto a website that promised "Ancient castles at reasonable prices! And if you order before the holiday rush, we will dig your moat for free!" In addition to being known for holding grudges, Vongrüber was also rather thrifty. Those were his foils: resentment and coupons. Did he need a castle? Probably not. A nice condo would have done fine. But the last guy that questioned Vongrüber on whether he "need[ed] the recently dug-up Mammoth skeleton for your rec room" found himself up to his neck where the massive creature had been chilling for 10,000 years. He will have his castle if he wants it—it is a free country.

He quickly called a realtor and zipped up the road to the highway toward the Royal district the very next day. She led him through a dozen castles during that appointment, but none really suited his needs. He wanted one with massive pillars and turrets overlooking a cliff, a downhill in front to give him the upper hand in case of siege, and at least three full-sized bathrooms. How could he throw a big party with any less? He did not want his guests waiting in line. Just because it was a medieval fortress did not mean it could not also be practical. That first day was a nice start but he scheduled another session about a week later with a different realtor. When he met with her, he got good vibes from her from the start as she had his sister's name: Helga. The sound of it smelled like a bouquet of morning blooms. It's a good German name.

She brought him around to another dozen, but to no avail. This was proving a fruitless venture, until she spotted one more not too far from the highway, pretty close to the gas station, which was convenient because there were not a lot of stations in this area with diesel and she needed to stop anyway to refuel.

They gassed up and zipped off to the last place on the map in this region. There was a "For Rent" sign out front, but the lights were off and the gong-style doorbell was broken. They waited a few minutes.

"Maybe they can hear the bell inside, and we just cannot hear it out front here," Helga posited.

Finally a small man opened the door. He barely exceeded five feet tall, but he did have some large pale eyes and a nice hunch going. He seemed trustworthy. He invited Vongrüber and Helga over the threshold and an oversized grandfather clock chimed loudly thirteen times in the foyer. Vongrüber did not like the ominous number of chimes, but Jens, the door gremlin, assured him that the clock ran on military time.

"Time for afternoon tea," Jens clapped his hands and the hallway light came on and an army of servants dressed to the nines in black tuxedos appeared to lead them into the sitting room. They sat and ate shortbread and drank a fine lavender tea with hints of local lemongrass, while Jens described the castle and its grounds. There were massive pillars and turrets overlooking a cliff, a downhill in front to give him the upper hand in case of siege, an enormous hedge maze on the eastern grounds (which had a bit of an unfortunate history, as one time during a party, a young guy named Jack got lost inside because he had had too many lavender teas and promptly froze to death), and three and a half bathrooms. This place was all Vongrüber could have asked for in a 16th century castle. But with all these wonderful amenities, he had become skeptical. "Why is this magnificent castle on the market? What's wrong with it?"

"Well," Jens leaned back on his chair and put his feet up on the floral ottoman, and scratched his chin. "There is nothing wrong with it. The master just decided he wanted to have a change of pace, really. The town is building a subway out here, and there are already enough noises that echo up these cliffs at night. And by renting, he still makes a chunk of change on the place. The only thing about the castle I do not like is the wood paneling in the basement. It feels cheap and I like to consider myself a trendy fellow."

"Wait, you are not the master of this castle?" Helga asked Jens.

"Me? Oh no! I could never afford this. This is a part-time job for me; I really want to be an actor, but this pays the bills."

"Where is the master today?" Vongrüber asked him.

"He's on a trip to Zurich at the moment. Should return in a few days' time."

"Would you call me as soon as he is back? I would like to discuss buying the place from him as opposed to renting."

"I'll ask him, but I think he is pretty set on leasing it. The neighborhood is improving and he wants to get his money's worth."

"His money's worth? Did he pay for the castle? This looks centuries old!"

"Irrelevant. It was his inheritance. It was originally owned by his great-great-grandfather, Chancellor Georg Gemütlichkeit."

"Your master is a Gemütlichkeit?!" Vongrüber almost fell out of his chair.

"Of course! He's the only remaining Gemütlichkeit in these parts. Supposedly there are a few left somewhere in Berlin or some such place, but they are a disgrace to the name Gemütlichkeit, like the mundane slobs they are."

Vongrüber frowned. "...My name is Vongrüber Gemütlichkeit. Whose great-great-great-uncle is Chancellor Georg Gemütlichkeit. Though I never knew the Liechtenstein Gemütlichkeits, my mother told me bedtime stories of my ancestors." Vongrüber changed his tone, "Because I adore the design and feel of the castle, I will pretend I did not hear you speak ill of my family. But you better mind your tongue as I will be a guest in this house henceforth."

"A guest? I am confused, you wanted to buy the place a minute ago..."

"Right. But I should like to get to know my kin on an intimate level, and in time who knows what will happen."

"I do not think the master will approve..."

"The master will be a good host. The Gemütlichkeits are famous for their hospitality. I will hear no more about it. Or you will not hear anything at all. Understand?"

Vongrüber stood up and shook the frightened door gremlin's hand and showed himself out with Helga hot on his heels. They sped down the hill and made a beeline for his home, where he began packing his things that night.

The very next morning, Vongrüber had his morning coffee and toast extra early, reading the paper faster than normal, and brushing his teeth haphazardly. He was excited to get to know the castle that would become his residence. He hopped into his old Volvo with the slight tear in the maroon driver's seat, and the brand new leather trim that replaced the passenger headrest from that Halloween when his friend Johan, dressed as a Viking, drunkenly turned on head banging music. Though the speakers had a bit of a tinny sound to them, music was pumping through Vongrüber's head, and he anxiously tapped his knuckles on the steering wheel while he tore through the Liechtenstein countryside.

Now on his drive, Vongrüber passed a small collective of poor and unfortunate "damned souls." He stopped his car suddenly, and in the rearview mirror, stared at the wandering mess of semi-dead folks trying to fill water from the well. These particular people were not as far gone as the average "damned soul." They were force-fed the cure like the rest. There was a difference with them though. Maybe there was not a high enough dosage, maybe they were too far gone, maybe it was just a knockoff brand of the drug. Regardless, these folks were only half back to normal. And when the moon shone fully every month, they would get aggressive and the neighboring towns would hear stories of vulgar creatures of the night coming out to tip their livestock, urinate on their crops, and sometimes both. They were like flesh-eating frat boys. Even though most of the time this group was in control, a half-Zed is still a Zed. At least in the eyes of Vongrüber Gemütlichkeit.

The music in his head subsided, but his fingers continued to tap on the dash irregularly to the constant sound of the Volvo's hazard lights. Remember, Vongrüber is not one to easily forget. But now was not the time, he knew. He had other places to be, other people to see. He put his car back in gear and once again sped off towards the Castle Gemütlichkeit.

He pulled up in the driveway of the castle and parked. With his blinkers blinking in full array, he pulled out a newspaper to pass the time. Not a few minutes later, a drip-drip-drip appeared on his windshield and he leaned out over his steering wheel to see dark clouds rolling in over the top of the castle. He pulled the wiper lever down once to clear the few drips, and stared at the clouds in a childlike wonder. These stratocumulus clouds blew in on quick winds and hovered like a hummingbird searching for nectar. The light grays transformed into a greenish sludge color and the drip-drip-drips became more constant, falling in stronger bursts and clumps, and Vongrüber once again calmly pulled the wiper lever, raised the soft-top of his Volvo, and put his paper down on the dash. As the rain fell harder and harder, Vongrüber got the feeling that this would not be the day he would meet the soon-to-be-former-host of Castle Gemütlichkeit. But he also was not willing to let those clouds rain on his parade, so he decided to take a walk.

*****

In that area of countryside, there was a weekly street fair. Well, not exactly a street fair, but not exactly a regular fair either—this was a fair off of the beaten path, but not roped and wrangled by fences as usual, and within striking distance of the highway. There were many fairs just like it along that stretch of road. This was the best way to feed the local economies since the fair vendors' towns were glorified campsites. They would sell lemonade and Schwarzwälder Kirsche. They had dunk tanks with the occasional Zed straggler that was just-this-side-too-dead to be reintegrated. They had petting zoos and horse drawn carriage rides. They were great fun. Except when it rained.

Vongrüber stumbled onto one of these fairs just as they started breaking down the bigger exhibits and tarping off the smaller ones. He ducked under a tent and sat in one of the folding chairs provided, while the vendors ran around making safe their gadgets and gear. He watched them with a slight smile, and pulled out his paper from under his arm to look nonchalant more than to actually read it.

One of the vendors who owned a massive (yet somehow portable) wood-burning stove from two towns over was having a great bit of trouble tarping it off as the winds roared over the adjacent hill and fought him when he tried to secure the ropes. Now, Vongrüber was not a rude man, and he decided he would make some use of himself on this day since his other plans were failing. He grabbed the flapping sail of plastic that kept evading the vendor, and pulled it down with the force of a longshoreman until it could be properly fastened to the spike dug in the muddy ground. The vendor threw a couple sand bags on top of the spike once it was secure for good measure and then shook Vongrüber's hand with gratitude.

"That would have been bad news if you had not stepped in, stranger. Thank you for that! This stove has been in my family for more than three generations and the weather 'round these hills is wearing and tearing the damn thing so much it may be decommissioned for good in the not too distant future. It needs a thorough refurbishing, I think. Damned rust bucket! Can't even get the funds to fix it is the worst part. These fairs have been interrupted by foul weather more than a few times these last months."

"How much are the repairs?" Vongrüber inquired with gears turning in his head.

"Let's just say this: a year of good fairs would fare me well. I am losing more money on horses dragging this devil around than I make baking with it."

"Is there an alternative to you fixing it?"

"What are you suggesting, sir?" the baker stopped tidying a moment and turned to Vongrüber.

"I am suggesting, how much would you sell it for?"

"Are you asking 'cause you are interested or because you are curious? I do not want to consider it unless we are talking numbers."

"We are talking numbers. The name is Gemütlichkeit by the way, Vongrüber. I am only ever interested in numbers."

"Of the Gemütlichkeits, from Castle Gemütlichkeit?"

"The same."

"Then the answer is no. Thanks for your help mein herr, but the Gemütlichkeits are.... let's just say I would sooner go hungry than help them... I have no problems with you but I disagree profoundly with the owner of Castle Gemütlichkeit. Good day." The baker continued battening down.

"Well, wait, let me start again. My name is Vongrüber Gemütlichkeit and yes, I belong to *that* clan. However, until yesterday I'd never been to this region, nor have I yet met Lord Gemütlichkeit."

"Regardless, sir..."

"Allow me to finish before you run away, let me go on please! Thank you. I am as much like Lord Gemütlichkeit as your now shoddy stove is to its original master's. If you bought butter that was left in the sun, is it the same as fresh butter in a fridge? No, one is spoiled and bitter and the other is rich and delicious. I am the delicious butter. I am fresh. And I am, if I had to describe myself as anything, a hobbyist. I find things I like and I pursue them," Vongrüber proudly puffed up his chest.

"This sounds more like the butter in the sun."

"Now listen here, sir, I am a good man with good intentions, and I want to do business with a business man. Now if I have to be subjected to your taunts much longer, my business will not be the only thing you will lose. Our conversation will conclude with a bow and a 'good day, ma'am,' if you catch my meaning. Now I am reasonable, if not generous, and I am interested in numbers more than words, so please, sir, quote me a number while I am still cheerful."

The vendor considered his words for a moment. Castration is not an ideal way to end a day, but there were no police in this region to beg for help should this Gemütlichkeit attack him.

"Are you even a baker?" he asked, already suspecting the answer.

"Does it matter?" Vongrüber's eyes were narrowing with each silly question.

"This is a fearsome piece of machinery..." The baker tried to back peddle now that it looked like he was not getting rid of the stranger.

"Fearsome? Pish posh! What is it going to take for you to quote me a number?"

Again the baker considered his options. "Well, let me offer a proposition... followed by a quote, if you will allow me?"

"Go on," Vongrüber said with intrigue as he rolled up his paper and tucked it under his arm. Counter offers to Vongrüber were like Happy Ending—they were not advertised, but dammit, they felt good.

"You say you are a good man..."

"I do not just say, I am a good man!" he retorted, losing patience.

"Yes, yes, you say you are a good man, and I can tell you are naught but a gentleman by your demeanor," the baker barbed, thanking God after he pulled his foot out of his mouth that Vongrüber was unfamiliar with sarcasm.

"So let me say this: I am, as you can plainly see, down on my luck, and you are, as I can plainly see a... hobbyist..." he cringed at the implications of that word, "who may or may not have experience with this type of machinery. If you can afford to buy this stove outright, with the knowledge that it will likely require thorough repairs to be up to snuff, then you can afford to hire me as its attendant and full-time bake master. I can keep it tuned up, and make you whatever you would like, and all I would require is a room to stay in with my trusty dog and the leftovers from your dinners. You need not even pay me wages. I have a lifetime of experience with this stove, and we can make you... very happy... I suspect." The baker hated himself for suggesting this. His siblings had been offered into indentured servitude and he never saw them again.

"So, let me get this straight. If I buy the stove at cost of the materials, and allow you to stay with me and feed you my scraps, you will work for me indefinitely and whenever I wish?" Vongrüber smiled as he spoke.

"These are hard times, Herr Gemütlichkeit."

"Apparently so," he stroked his chin where his beard would be if he could grow it. "When could this happen?" He suddenly got excited.

"Well, I would like to sell my house first if possible, and have my possessions ready to move. This way we could do it all in a hurry."

"I would like to make moves in a month. Could you sell by then?"

"Hopefully so. I cannot make someone buy my house, but I can make a strong effort to sell."

"I am trying to buy Lord Gemütlichkeit's castle from him, and he was not around today, but I am hoping within the next couple days he will arrive and I can persuade him to see things my way."

"What do you mean? That sounds rather precarious," the baker became nervous.

"I'm not going to pillage the man, Bakemaster—he is looking to lease the place, I want to persuade him to sell. So I own the place. You understand."

"Of course. Out of curiosity, why do you want that castle? This region has more Zeds than most."

"You are most observant. It is a beautiful piece of architecture, and as you just stated: *more Zeds than most*," Vongrüber again stroked his chin.

"I'm confused, Herr."

"All will become clear. Sell your home and ring me when you do." He handed the baker a business card then reached for his hand and shook it firmly twice, and without another word or backwards glance, walked from the security of the tent back down the road to his car parked at the castle.

*****

Another two days passed before the Lord returned home. Vongrüber was already there when the Lord pulled up in his vintage Rolls Royce. As always, Vongrüber put down his paper on the dash. He checked his hair in the rearview, and greeted the Lord from a distance.

Lord Gemütlichkeit, however, had not spoken to his door gremlin or checked his messages and was not aware anyone would be coming, so he was particularly surprised when he saw someone that shared his likeness briskly walking towards him with business on his mind.

"Who the hell are you?" the Lord asked with a gruff timbre in his voice. Vongrüber stopped suddenly. He had not expected him to sound like that with a figure so dainty. For a moment, he thought another man was hidden behind a tree and spoke for him; that he was being fooled. The Lord sounded like a seasoned woodsman who knew the subtleties in a good whiskey, who likely went through a bulk pack of pipe tobacco in an evening, who could reminisce about that time he strangled an eleven foot tall brown bear that interrupted his morning tea on his patio. He was dressed exquisitely in designer metropolitan fashions, from his hair product to his luxury moccasins. He was highly irregular.

The Lord spoke again, "Who the hell are you and why are you in my driveway?"

Vongrüber started moving again. They were related after all. He needed to have courage if he was going to muscle this dragon from his keep.

"My Lord," he bowed to him but quickly uprighted himself, "my name is Vongrüber Gemütlichkeit, I am of your lineage and I hail from Berlin. I have travelled many miles to visit with you and to inquire about your castle."

"Next time skip the intro, I am only interested in the lease. Please come in." The Lord extended his arm, welcoming Vongrüber into his home. *That seemed too easy*, he thought as he crossed the threshold passing Jens in the doorway. As they sat in his smoking room, the Lord offered him a piece of shortbread to go with his cappuccino.

"So how did you come to find this castle? Were you wandering down memory lane and stumbled onto another Gemütlichkeit or is that coincidence? Are you as much a business man as I?" The Lord inquired with a subtle proud smile on his lips.

"Merely a coincidence I will admit." Vongrüber suddenly felt his shoulders hunch over and his voice grow softer. "Though I was in the market for a castle exactly like yours. I suppose style runs in the family." He forced a chuckle, but the Lord just stared at him.

"Well I was not even aware that there were any of us left. Just me. Jens tells me he gave you a tour the other day. Tell me, you said this was exactly what you were looking for in a castle; answer me two questions:

why does a common man like yourself want a castle? And why a castle like this one? It is beautiful, no doubt. But many are. This castle is right between *nowhere* and *somewhere*, with wandering Zeds pervading the hills nearby. Wouldn't you prefer the *nowhere* or the *somewhere* to the *in-between*?"

"Well, the style of your residence is on par with my exact specifications. I had looked all afternoon several days back, and the places I found lacked this... charm," he said looking up at the ceilings which fell into darkness, they were so high. The many animal heads mounted to the walls had solid white marbles where the eyes once lived, and the sounds of Jens grinding espresso beans and brewing another pot downstairs reverberated off the great stone walls, making the heads seem to roar subtly in the recesses of the room.

"So, besides the style, what about the latter point I mentioned? The Zeds?" The Lord dipped some shortbread into his cappuccino.

"Well, they do not scare me so much. In fact, I would prefer to keep my enemies close," Vongrüber felt his confidence returning.

"Why do you call them your enemies? Most have been pacified to whatever extent. Sure they might jump you on the road, which would be a great nuisance, but *enemy* is a strong word, my little Gemütlichkeit."

"I had an encounter with them as a boy when the war was in full swing."

"Ahh," said the Lord taking a sip of his coffee. He placed the mug down on the coaster and stood up to stretch his stiff legs. "How long are you looking to lease for?"

"That is the next point I was getting to," said Vongrüber also climbing to his feet, though his shaking knees were less than thrilled about the activity.

"Yes?"

"I wanted to see if you would sell me the place," he blurted out less elegantly than he would have liked.

"And why should I do that, Gemütlichkeit?"

"I want to start a new life here, and it seems like fate that I should come across your castle of all the castles in Liechtenstein."

"As I am sure Jens explained to you, this castle is being *leased* exclusively. That is the scenario. It is not being "leased or best offer." It is not being bartered or given. The thing it is especially not is 'for sale,'" the Lord stated coldly. Vongrüber swallowed hard, and noticed just how dry his throat felt. *Would it kill Jens to turn on a humidifier?*

"As Jens also explained to me, you are interested in getting out before the subway is completed. The noises are too much, echoing off the cliffs, or some silly thing," Vongrüber offered.

"That is true, but there is still a decent amount of time before they finish, so I am in no hurry to sell. You cannot hustle me. And furthermore, if I waited till the trains arrived, do you not think I could make even more leasing when this castle is hooked to the grid? An accessible castle is a profitable castle."

"Fair enough, but should the Zeds continue to overrun the area what makes you think anyone would lease the place?"

"I had that same thought. Funny you should mention that. That will not be a problem in a month's time, though."

"Sorry?" Vongrüber did not like the way this was going.

"If you had a mouse problem, would you just tough it out? No, that is where the plague came from in the first place. I would not abide it for a moment longer than necessary. Neither would you. Especially if it stood in the way of a plentiful revenue stream."

"You are going to wipe them out?!" Vongrüber sat down again, realizing that he was shouting.

"Righto, boy. And why shouldn't I?" the Lord smiled. Vongrüber bit his lip. Apparently Gemütlichkeits think alike. He could not rightly call up humanitarian forces to shut down the Lord's plans if he was going to turn around and do the same thing. If he made a big deal of it to the authorities, upon his own genocide he would be shut down as well. Castle Gemütlichkeit would fall victim to eminent domain. It would become a museum and the Zeds would be memorialized as victims of the cruel Gemütlichkeits.

"Why, indeed?" Vongrüber tried to think of something to do, anything to stop the massacre... so he himself could spearhead it.

"No thoughts?"

"How could I rebut? I can ask you nicely to reconsider?" his voice was even softer than before.

"And I can reiterate, that you can reconsider your intent and lease from me, or Jens can reiterate where the door is."

Vongrüber was not easily beaten but he was outsmarted on this go-round. He sipped his cappuccino and nibbled on his shortbread like a soggy bunny. For several moments he did this staring at the floor, but he could feel the Lord looking at him with a big maniacal grin. He could hear the ruffling of the Lord petting the wild boar's coarse hair mounted near the fireplace. The Lord was content to watch Vongrüber squirm, he needed not chat.

"Do you have any appointments to show the place?" Vongrüber finally asked to break the silence.

"Not this week or next. There may be a man coming from Cape Town next month depending on his schedule," the Lord lit up a cigar with an ivory butane lighter.

"Changing gears slightly, Lord, would you allow me to stay here out of familial goodness to gauge how I feel about the place? It is a pretty large castle, and I can stay out of your way if you would prefer... but this way I can see if I would be willing to lease from you...with my proverbial tail between my legs?" Vongrüber cringed saying that aloud. "And should no lease come of it, I can clear off before your Cape Town visitor arrives."

"Ooo, I like that: lease from me with your tail between your legs. That is the kind of deal I can get behind. But what do I gain in the meantime?" Vongrüber tried to think of what he could offer a man with everything.

"Well... I am getting a Bakemaster in the near future, what if I brought him and his massive vintage wood burning stove to Castle Gemütlichkeit, and he can serve you while he serves me?"

"I have a cook already. What good is this man's stove?"

"It is generations old, and he has a lifetime of experience with it. He can make delicious desserts and breads and whatever you would like I am sure. You can lay off your wait staff awhile and save money on cooks, while we decide what to do about this deal. What say you?"

"What indeed? Well I say this firstly: I am fond of my cook. That said, I am not opposed to a month of reduced expenses." He sat down and weighed his options.

"So what say you? I stay here with my Bakemaster, and you get one month less of food expenditures and a possible lessee." Now it was the Lord's turn to nibble his shortbread and sip on his cappuccino. There were several minutes of the sounds of firewood crackling under the chimney and abrasive sneezing by Vongrüber—who was apparently allergic to boar's hair when he tried to pet the beast's head himself.

The Lord had come to a decision, and standing up he said, "One month, you may stay. We can chat at meals, and if we pass each other in the bathroom. Otherwise you mind your business and I will mind mine. One month from now, when the man from Cape Town arrives you are already gone unless you have signed the lease."

Without another word, they shook each other's hands firmly twice, and Vongrüber exited the building to go and find his baker. He hopped in his car and with a roar of the engine, gunned it down the highway. At once he was filled with excitement and terror. He flipped on the radio to distract his mind. "Sunshine Lollipops" erupted through his speakers, and he said to himself, "I can work with this."

*****

He swerved his Volvo back and forth across the highway avoiding Zeds to the poppy sounds of Leslie Gore—an apt surname he thought, given the scenery. In a hurry, he pulled up outside of the baker's house and honked five or twelve times and bolted from his car to stand on the doorstep. The baker emerged, terrified. "Herr Gemütlichkeit, you are back so soon!"

"Shut up, baker, what is the status on the property...is it sold?"

"Sold? It has been two days, and I have barely gotten the chance to find a realtor." Vongrüber's face dropped like the mayor's pants at a whorehouse. "Given the urgency of this deal, how long do you realistically require?"

"...Maybe a week or two? If I push..."

"Yes yes, you must push. I need this to go through yesterday." He began pacing.

"Uhhh...." muttered the baker.

"Think!" Vongrüber screamed to himself. The baker was taken aback and fell silent.

"Don't be like a kicked puppy, you idiot, that was at me." He paced up and back the steps in front of the home, and started mumbling silly things to himself. The baker kept his back to the house; his eyes ping ponging as Herr Gemütlichkeit began to resemble a wolf on the road with mange and an unhealthy caffeine addiction.

"Well dammit, we will just need to put this deal through and I will sell it later," he finally articulated, and the baker, sensing his attention returning his direction, shuddered and put his hands up in defense as Gemütlichkeit rushed up to him.

"Baker. Go fetch the deed and whatever change purse you can find in your damned hovel, there's no time to lose." The baker, still hunched over without a clue as to what was happening, started to speak, but Gemütlichkeit took his rolled up newspaper and made quick work of the baker's nose.

"Bakemaster! Fetch your purse; I'll fill it! And bring me the deed, for the deal is done. Fetch!"

The baker ran into his home and pulled out the deed, carefully lifted his piggy bank from off his nightstand, and before leaving, grabbed a few photos from their frames around his home. He returned to find Vongrüber honking furiously in the driver's seat of his Volvo. The baker whistled and his dog came running from around the house to his owner's side. The trunk popped and the baker placed his goods and a travel bag into the back of the car, and took his seat alongside his new master and his faithful canine. The car peeled out of the driveway, and the baker stole one last look at his mother's house that her father had built for her with his own hands. He sighed and slumped down in the seat.

Music blaring, Gemütlichkeit again swerved between Zeds, honking to the beat. Periodically he would see neighboring folks walking to town or from restaurants on the outskirts, and he made a thorough point of explaining exactly where he was going. In his loudest voice possible he shouted, "STAYING WITH MY FAMILY AT THE OLD GEMÜTLICHKEIT CASTLE, TRA LA LA! FAMILY REUNIONS ARE SO JOYOUS! DID YOU KNOW THE LORD IS SICK? I HAVE TO TAKE CARE OF HIM. WHAT A SAD CIRCUMSTANCE TO REUNITE WITH FAMILY, AYE?"

Now aiming for the center of town, he again repeated his obnoxiously loud rant to anyone in earshot, to the point that an officer of the law pulled him over in a hurry, citing him for creating a public disturbance. But not before finding out that Lord Gemütlichkeit is ill and is too embarrassed to speak of it. Word spread through town of his illness, but not to the Lord himself, who was of course as healthy as adolescent glue... that is, as a horse.

As Vongrüber and the reluctant baker sped toward the castle, the Lord Gemütlichkeit found himself mysteriously getting free goods and services in town from a bunch of pitying merchants. "Your dry cleaning is on the house, sir. Take care now!" said the Cleaner, tipping his hat with his brow tightened. *The Lord has been some of my best business—pity it will be to see him go.*

"Now do not be silly, I can afford the cost, how much do I owe?" He said flabbergasted at the fourth merchant to give him inexplicable treatment. "Your smile is enough, sir. Be well!" He tipped his hat again. The Lord sighed, thanking the cleaner and returning to his car to find the local Hobo polishing his windows.

"Dammit, I do not need my windows cleaned, thank you but please stop, I do not have any change for you!"

"Oh, this is on the tarp, sir."

"The tarp? What are you saying?"

"Well the expression is 'on the house' but given my circumstances, sir... Regardless, I wanted to do you a kindness," the Hobo tipped his hole-riddled hat as well.

"What the bloody hell is going on here!? I do not need kindnesses! I am perfectly able to pay for cleaning, or car washing, or butchery, or shoe shinery! Why are you doing this? Did I miss some special law get signed where the elite get everything 'on the tarp!?'"

"This isn't America, sir. Hope you are well!" The Hobo began to skip down the road. Aggravated, the Lord pulled out his wallet and caught up to the Hobo, handing him a $100 bill.

"Nobody takes these in town anyway, may it better serve you than me, Lester. You be well, and let everyone else know that they should stop telling me to be well: I AM well."

"A *well* of kindness, good Lord!" He skipped away.

"Achhhh!" He drove home in his spotless car, where he found Vongrüber and a dirty looking man with an old bloodhound sitting on his stoop.

"Well well well, back already? And if it isn't the Bakemaster I have heard so much about. What is your name, Bakemaster?" A moment of silence.

"I am sorry, did you ask my name?"

"Of course silly creature, what is your name? Are you hard of hearing?" demanded the Lord.

"Not hard of hearing sir, it's just, not even Vongrü..." Vongrüber punched his arm with a glare. "Sorry. Herr Gemütlichkeit. Not even the Herr has asked for my name."

Vongrüber laughed embarrassed, and he turned to the Lord. "I've asked him his name, what a stupid thing to say, his name is... Winchester."

"My name is Georg." The Lord marveled to himself: *Georg! Just like great-great-grandfather, the Chancellor!*

"Yes, yes, you did not let me finish, Georg Winchester," interjected Vongrüber.

"Kleinmann. Georg Kleinmann."

"Bakemaster, I am tired of your interruptions, Georg Kleinmann Winchester, now speak no more of this!"

After Vongrüber turned away, the baker whispered under his breath, "Not a Winchester. That's English."

"Vongrüber, please stop harassing Georg. He is a guest in this home, as much as you, and I am sure he will prove far more useful than you, so put a lid on that pot," the Lord said with a tired look on his face.

"Lord, we have come a long way, and I have two requests, followed by a service to you: 1) Can I use your bathroom? and 2) Can we put our bags in our rooms? Then Lord, I will take you to see the brilliant bronze oven that shall make you fine meals to come!" Vongrüber proclaimed.

"Yes yes, use the toilet."

The Lord knocked heartily on the bathroom door and Jens came out. "Master! It is great to see you."

"Lead Vongrüber and the charming Georg..." he said staring at Vongrüber smugly, "to their rooms to put down their bags, then kindly escort Vongrüber to the lavatory. Thank you." Vongrüber and Georg climbed to their feet and grabbed their luggage.

"Oh and Von—I will be calling you Von henceforth, Vongrüber is so long winded—please wipe your feet on the mat before entering." Vongrüber resented both of those statements. But he had to relieve himself more. So with a frown, he wiped his feet and followed Jens. *Soon things would change.*

*****

An hour later, they were coasting through the countryside, Vongrüber at the helm of his Volvo and the Lord sitting shotgun, obviously getting carsick amid all the swerving around the Zeds. Townsfolk saw him riding, holding on for dear life, looking pale and a little green, and crossed themselves. "Poor, poor man, all the good he has done. I hope he pulls through."

Finally the Volvo came to a clearing as the sun began to set, but storm clouds began rolling in. They climbed out of the car.

"Well Von, where the hell are we?"

Knowing exactly where, he turned to his baker. "Winchester!"

"It's Georg."

"What did I say about that?! Dammit Winchester, where are we? What have you done with your oven?"

"We passed the fairgrounds some time back... master."

"And you did not say so?! You wretched little man! Lord, I am terribly sorry for Winchester's failure to direct us."

Raindrops started to fall, slowly at first, but picking up rapidly, creating a mess of puddles and disheveled roads behind the car.

"Curses! The roads are soaked, and this car only has rear wheel drive! There is only one way to get to the fairgrounds now! We must walk along this path here! That will take us where we need to go! Come along!"

"Oh Von, I am never a victim of circumstance." The Lord removed a rectangular remote box from his vest pocket and pressed the button labeled, "Emergency."

"What? Why??" Vongrüber shrieked.

"We have sturdy vehicles at the castle that can weather the weather. What good is walking to the fairgrounds anyway if we cannot pull the blasted stove home with us?"

An intercom on the remote clicked on, "Yes, sir? How can I be of help?"

"Jens! Good man. Track my beacon and come get us please..."

"The Humvee or the Rolls, sir?"

"Yes, the Humvee."

"The yellow or the black?" Jens asked nonchalantly.

"No no, the yellow one, it increases our visibility in the storm. Thank you Jens," he pressed the button again disconnecting the intercom.

"See, now we just sit back and wait." He walked back to the car and put the roof up as the rain began to pour. Georg shrugged at Von, and followed in tow. The car, now sealed up, began pumping cheerful music. Vongrüber was so close to his sneaky plan coming to fruition only to forget that billionaires do not follow other people's plans. He stomped his feet in a rage.

"Well dammit all! I DO follow plans. Jens will not be of any help... Jens!" He stomped again, getting mud on his shirt.

He slipped and sloshed as he moseyed up the hill and along the path to find a biker gang of Zeds sitting in their torn up leather vests and chaps.

"Oyy! You there!" He slid down the hill towards them. There were five of them, all obviously terrifying in a former life, but now after being Zeddified for a few years, they were about as burly and tough as a bag boy at the local mart. They were teaching each other phonics again, using colorful flashcards with rounded edges and sounding out words. But there were five of them. And they had not eaten in awhile.

"Oyyy!" Von knocked the cards out of the Zed's hand. "Stop trying to better yourself, you are filthy and silly and your accents are atrocious! It is not pronounced 'woooed': wood is pronounced 'woōd', similar to "would... you stop with that because you are embarrassing yourself, you mongrel."

"That was so rude! Pronounced 'roōd,'" the toughest looking biker Zed retorted.

"You know what else is roōd? This!" Vongrüber gave the biggest biker Zed a wedgie.

"Owww!! Why woōd you do that? Was your mother an ogre?"

"My mother was a lovely lady!" Vongrüber said suddenly getting defensive.

"So why don't you marry her?" said the wedgied Zed, chuckling at his own wit.

"Dammit!" He slapped each of them in the face. "Bet you can't catch me!" He ran back up the hill towards the car, falling twice on his face. He ducked behind a tree, waiting for them to come over the hill and rip the Lord to shreds. Several moments passed, however, and no gang of bikers.

"What the..." He looked over the hill and they had gone back to studying phonics. Lying on his stomach, he started throwing rocks at them to provoke them.

"Would you kindly cut that out?" one shouted at him. "It's hard enough to re-enter society without proper grammar, but I really do not need one more bump or bruise on my head."

"And yes, I *am* hungry," shouted another at him, "but I would rather not eat junk food," he high-fived the other Zeds, each of them cheering him on.

The rain picked up, covering Vongrüber with increasingly more mud. from the hill. The Zeds obviously would not help. He put down the rock he was about to throw at them and had an epiphany. He looked at the same rock. Then himself. He was disgusting. And unrecognizable. The gears in his head spun into place, and he lifted the rock and walked to the driver's side of the car. He opened the door and pulled the Lord out by his collar, grunting loudly in his best Zed imitation. He then proceeded to hit the Lord with the rock until he fell limp. Georg ducked under the seat screaming, covering his head. *For such a cold blooded act on a distant family member, I honestly feel pretty removed from him,* Vongrüber thought to himself, amused he could make puns and murder at the same time... *I could be a Bond villain!*

Von removed his keys and wallet and any other valuable resources from the Lord's pockets, then dragged his corpse to the top of the hill and rolled him down. "How 'bout this as a peace offering! A nice *rich* meal!" He chuckled to himself, and the Lord rolled to a stop at their feet. They saw his fine clothing and realized who he was and knew what they would do! They knelt over his lifeless body...and!... Each shed a tear for him. They said a few words and started digging him a grave for a proper Lutheran burial.

"What the whatting what what!??" Vongrüber screamed out. Pounding his fists into the mud. "Damn, damn, damn, damn, damn!!"

At last, he collected himself. The storm still pounded away, and he thought to himself, *the deed is done regardless of the way it was done.* He rinsed off as much mud as he could and returned to his car. Georg was still screaming in fear. "Cut that out, and help me put chains on the tires."

He popped the trunk and removed his vehicle safety kit, pulling out three tire chains. *Apparently one has gone missing. Damn.* Georg arrived at his side, and helped him chain the tires, and they sputtered away at a snail's pace.

"The upholstery has seen better days," he said to Georg, who was still shivering in fear and sadness at the events that had just transpired, "am I right? ... Yep, better days."

They parked at the castle and Vongrüber keyed into the front door. Stripping down and leaving his filthy clothes on the stoop, he went up to his new castle office and searched for the number of a locksmith.

"Yep, bring a partner or two," he spoke into the phone, "there are a lot of locks that need changing." Then he called the sheriff and explained that he had not seen the Lord since their walk a few hours before and feared for the worst, as the yellow Humvee had gone missing... though he had the tracking coordinates from the truck. The officers were on the scene in a matter of minutes, and they did in fact find the yellow Humvee on the site of a recently dug grave with a ranting and raving Jens who was not cooperating with them. Suffice it to say, it caused a stir in town. The news vans arrived on the scene and the whole area was broadcast to the town.

Vongrüber kicked his feet up in the tub, surrounded by vanilla candles and bubbles galore, and watched on the bathroom television as Jens was dragged away in a paddy wagon. *Not a bad day's work.* He sipped champagne from the wine cellar. Master hobbyist turned castle owner in an afternoon. And all it cost was a pittance for the baker's crappy house.

Three days later, after an investigation proved that the Lord's body was covered in Zed DNA as well as Jens'—who always took the lint roller to his master's suits—Vongrüber gave the eulogy at his funeral and pledged to the hundreds of townspeople that attended that he would see justice for the fallen Lord. He promised.

*****

Twelve months hence to the day, with no public word from Vongrüber since the funeral, the Castle Gemütlichkeit opened a restaurant on the grounds with a promise of great food at even better prices. Featured prominently in the center of the "Casa Gemütlichkeit" (sounds commercial, no?) was the Bakemaster's brilliantly polished and refurbished copper oven shining under the track lighting. The Bakemaster, Georg Kleinmann Von Winchester Gemütlichkeit—or so said his nametag to keep the brand pure—proudly made delicious breads and cakes and desserts aplenty. And though business was doing well, the masterwork was not yet unveiled.

The restaurant was the talk of the town, and word of its greatness had extended so far that a special dinner had been arranged for the Royal family of Liechtenstein as well as a committee of Michelin critics.

Vongrüber's mission following the acquisition of the castle was to render other restaurants obsolete. "Casa Gemütlichkeit" had been working on and perfecting a special dish in memoriam of the fallen Lord for the year since the funeral, since the moats surrounding the castle began filling with random Zeds from all nearby regions. The dish was comprised of several elements, all of which needed to be cooked well done so as to rid the meat of parasites, but would be served in a unique faux-ivory vessel each and every time. This recipe had been slaved over and was being kept under lock and key until the big unveiling at the special dinner only a few days away.

In preparation for the unveiling, Vongrüber asked Bakemaster Georg Kleinmann Von Winchester Gemütlichkeit to have one last taste testing for him, to guarantee the flawlessness of the dish. He had grown nervous in the weeks since he heard the Michelin folks and the Royals were set to visit and required perfection while dining. After this unveiling, he would retire his self-descriptor as "hobbyist" and embrace his new title: *Lord Gemütlichkeit*. He was sure he would be knighted. He was convinced of it.

When the clock struck nine on the evening of the taste test, he sat down as he had countless times at the grand dining table in his glorious castle, surrounded by shimmering silver cutlery and glorious bronze and gold statuettes of the line of Gemütlichkeits before him on the mantelpiece. In fact, there was a big spot on the wall that would soon be filled with the next Lord's portrait: the successor to the line of Gemütlichkeits. Vongrüber was so confident about the dinner that he arranged for a painter to come the day after the unveiling.

As he so often had, Georg entered the room dressed to the nines in a pristine velvet suit, carrying a silver tray with its accompanying silver lid. Vongrüber skipped the salad this evening: the main course would be his only course. Georg placed the tray in front of Vongrüber and lifted the lid, releasing a cloud of billowing steam. He removed the dish from the tray and retreated to the kitchen where he set the tray down on the countertop. In front of Vongrüber sat his masterpiece: a full Zed head with the cap of the dome removed precisely, bone polished with boiling water prior, and the cooked cranial meat exposed above the dome, seasoned to perfection. This was what he had envisioned in his mind's eye since his sister had lost her thumbs when they were children. Revenge was a dish best served cold... or in this case, hot, as Zed brains needed to be thoroughly cooked because they might still carry the virus.

He breathed it in. It was elegant. The aromas filled his own brain with wonder, and with their careful tinkering of the recipe, it also had umami! Vongrüber lifted his fork and knife and cut into the meat. Despite its doneness, it remained tender and juicy. He lifted it to his mouth and bit down, savoring every molecule of it. Georg could hear moans of delight through the kitchen door, and watched through the little window as his master consumed their creation.

When the Zed was all gone, he asked Georg to bring him a cordial and a cigarette as well as some lady fingers. After Georg vanished into the kitchen, Vongrüber chuckled at his order's irony and put his feet up on the edge of the enormous table. Georg placed his drink, smoke, and snacks in front of him and he drank and smoked and nibbled until he had consumed his fill, then relocated to his sitting room where he regularly listened to music in the evenings.

But as "Sunshine Lollipops" echoed off of his castle's walls, he felt a little strange. His stomach started rumbling and he was a touch sleepy. Normally this only happened when he ordered pizza or put too many ingredients into his omelets. *How many times do I need to tell myself, omelets should be simple and should not have more than two add-ons!* No matter, he would try to sleep it off, and laid down in his bed. It was probably nerves for the big night.

He slept all through the next day, and woke up groggy and dehydrated. He wobbled down the stairs and called for Georg. No answer. *He is probably on a run.* Vongrüber splashed some water on his face in the bathroom, but noticed some discoloration in his face. He was extra pale this morning and had minor scabs around his eyes and mouth. *Did Georg and I box last night? Did I fall making an omelet? What the devil happened?* He took a cold shower and hobbled back up to bed, feeling a fever coming on.

He awoke the next morning, on the day of the grand reveal for the Michelins and the Royals, and he looked terrible. Even more pale, even more scabs. He was at a loss.

"Georg!" His voice echoed off of the stone walls. No sounds whatsoever. He hobbled down the stairs with his comforter around his shoulders and looked around the grounds when he noticed smoke coming from the chimney in "Casa Gemütlichkeit" and realized, "IDIOT! Of course that is where he has been! Loyal servant! He was making everything ready for tonight!" He hobbled into the "Casa" and the front hall lights were off, but a few rays from the kitchen beamed through the circular windows in the doors and sounds of pots banging and boiling could be heard through the cracks. He went in. "There you are, Georg! I have been looking for you!"

"Oh good! You are here; I was just about to come find you. Oh dear, sir, you look awful, are you feeling okay?" Georg feigned concern as his master leaned against the doorpost.

"I feel bloody awful! I have a fever, I'm pale, and there are scabs everywhere. Wooooed you walk me back?" He stopped himself. Something about what he just said was wrong. His internal sirens went off. "Did I just ask you, 'wooooed you walk me?'"

"Why, yes, you did. You really look out of it, sir. I shall carry you back," Georg grabbed onto his master and steered him out of the kitchen, but Vongrüber could not keep his balance anymore and fell under his own weight. Georg lifted him over his shoulder and brought him to the grand bathroom and ran him a hot bath.

"Now I will be back shortly, you just relax." Georg disappeared and Vongrüber settled into the soothing water and felt himself getting sleepy again. He closed his eyes and nodded off a few times, then passed out. His body went limp in the bath.

The water, it turned out, was getting gradually warmer and warmer, and hotter and hotter. This was a method Georg learned from his mother. When preparing shellfish, she would tell him, put them into comfortable water, then turn the heat up. They will fall asleep and their meat will not tense up in the boiling water. This was the ultimate way to keep your meat tender.

By the time Georg returned, his master—*former master*—had expired at last and was ready to be prepared. Georg put on his chef's hat and coat and got to work, wearing his first smile for a very long time.

*****

The Michelin folks and the Royals sat around a large round table and served themselves cuts from the perfectly shined dome. It was impeccable. Perfectly cooked, perfectly tender. And had umami! This was a dish for the ages.

Upon word that Casa Gemütlichkeit was a newly minted Three Star Michelin establishment, with the approval of the Royals, Georg was promptly knighted and became heir to the castle and dubbed Lord Georg Kleinmann Von Winchester Gemütlichkeit, Noble Chef. He sat for his portrait, and hung it in the blank space on the wall in the dining room, as the latest in the long line of Gemütlichkeits. In a matter of days, Georg went from pauper to prince, defeating his own poverty and shame. And though he was dead,

Vongrüber too had his victory and won out over the scourge of the damned like he had always wanted. For when you have been wronged, always remember: revenge is a dish best served cold... but sometimes hot.

"SuperMarkt"

Oct 29, 2012 — Long Island City, NYC

"Gerald! We need to go!"

"Sergeant Mixtape's making pee-pee. Two more minutes!"

"Sergeant Mixtape's pee-pee is gonna ruin everything, get his ass in the car!"

"You're not going to like it when he wets the seats!"

"Then get him a bottle and a funnel! We have one in the cabinet! There's a small window before everything is going to be gone, and the storm is coming now!"

"Look, he's shaking it out! Just a second!"

"Ughhhhh!" Meredith stomped on the hardwood floor in her Long Island City apartment, and stormed off towards the door.

"I'm going to get the car, meet me downstairs in two minutes. If you're late, you're walking!" She slammed the door.

"Come on little buddy, pee faster!" Gerald looked at his adorable toy poodle with pleading eyes, and Sergeant Mixtape looked up at him as if to say, *I know, I'm going! Jesus!*

Finally the little stream dried up, and Gerald brought the dog back inside from the balcony and slid the door shut, just as the wind picked up and the 3' x 3' pee potty artificial lawn was hurdled from the balcony onto the street below. He opened the balcony door again to try and grab it, but it had dropped right onto the hood of his and Meredith's Audi below.

"GERALD!!!" Meredith shouted through the open car window. She triggered the wipers, and the pee slid back and forth on the windshield until the stream of blue fluid shot up from the washer canons and created a green slush before finally washing away the filth.

Gerald ran downstairs faster than he'd run since his Cross Country days in Connecticut half a decade prior when he met Meredith at the Torch Club in Greenwich. Meredith's eyes glowed like a dragon.

"Get in. Now." He slid in and didn't make eye contact. She slammed her door and the two sat in silence as she drove to the SuperMarkt near the river. As they pulled up out front, the line to get in had already grown to well over fifty people. She turned slowly to her cowering husband, and her pupils bore a hole straight through his skull.

"Do you want to tackle that line, or hit the main store?" he asked, refusing to acknowledge the Medusa gaze.

"I am so angry at you right now." She wielded her slow and surgical tone in the way that always made Gerald fold immediately. But time was short, so Gerald glossed over his usual thorough apology.

"Which line? In or out? This storm is coming, the radar on my watch says we have maybe fifteen minutes before the downpour makes landfall." She snapped out of her rage, and focused up.

"In."

"In it is, let's go."

They climbed out of the car, and Meredith bolted through the SuperMarkt's automatic doors, while Gerald handed the keys of his green sludge racing striped two-seater to the store's valet and got in the enormous line to the auxiliary shop adjacent.

He counted the minutes, and crosschecked the radar. *Fourteen minutes. Thirteen minutes.* The line slid a bit. *Twelve minutes.* The clouds rolled in even thicker and darker than before. *Eleven minutes.* Another ten feet crawled by. With ten minutes before Hurricane Sandy's fury hit the formerly industrial neighborhood, Gerald estimated he had around thirty feet more of line before he'd be covered by the awning. The in and out was steady—fortunately this particular store was highly regulated in times of crisis.

Five minutes. He'd only moved another ten feet since last he checked. *Two minutes.* A crack of thunder was heard from across the river, following a particularly strong bolt of lightning striking the Chrysler Building. "Come on. Come on. Almost there. Come on..."

One minute. He watched the radar line up over his head, and imagined himself sitting directly under the tractor beam of an alien spaceship. The air pressure dropped dramatically and a cold gust of air pushed inwards towards the store. With forty-five seconds remaining before the water would plunge from the skies, twenty customers rushed out of the store clutching their reusable shopping bags like they had just got the last rations from the UN before the warlords could ransack them. *This is it! I'm going to make it!*

As the line accelerated to the door, an older woman, probably mid to late seventies, dropped her bag and the six pack divider of various red and white wines plummeted and shattered in the entry way.

"Everyone take a step back!" shouted the SuperMarkt security official guarding the entrance like a diligent troll. "We need a mop to the front, ASAP!" His walkie buzzed some inaudible gibberish and a teen from the neighborhood, decked out in bright orange safety gear, ran to the front with his yellow roller bucket and mop outstretched like a lance. As the teen worked quickly to mop up the mess, the skies opened up, and Gerald looked to the heavens just in time to get saturated from tip to toe. One minute later, the old lady was cleared from the entrance and Gerald was allowed passage into the SuperMarkt Wine Store.

It was as cold a day as they come. It was late October, and yet the store still left their air conditioner on full blast. Gerald knew he'd get pneumonia, or TB, or one of those terrible diseases cable news constantly warns him about. His clothes dripped onto the marble linoleum and he left massive puddles behind him as he began his search.

This store was the busiest right before hurricanes. Famously. Every year. Today was the Black Friday for Alcoholics. But neither Gerald nor Meredith thought of themselves as *alcoholics*. This power couple was a pair of self-proclaimed "socialites," a term Meredith read on her Kindle and applied to their lives. Her drink of choice was anything white, but Gerald hated white wines... except for one rare bottle by a small vineyard in Vermont. The name was Chateau

Clouseau. It was a white but had a hint of rosé in it, giving it a fresh summery bouquet. For this reason, Chateau Clouseau was near impossible to find in October.

Most of their friends preferred dark reds with exotic berries and spices, and even some pumpkin thrown in for good measure, and though he loved those fancy weird wines, Meredith insisted they share because she wasn't a drunk. Even though they'd safely polish off two bottles to their lonesome in one sitting. Never mind that. If he was going to maintain order in this time of panic, he needed two things: a white to share, and a good story to make Meredith forgive him for the dog offense. Otherwise this would be one long stormed-in excursion.

With the dozens of high shelves and roller ladders connected at the top of aisles, and the store closing in thirty minutes, Gerald knew he'd be in for one helluva time. There was no time to lose.

*****

Meredith was scouring the SuperMarkt for seven very important items. Now this was a premium super store, so they would have everything... if they had anything. With the storm now raging outside, and the store nearing the closing hour, pretty much the whole supply had been ransacked. It was a ghost town. All the cashiers were open, but there were no customers in sight. Many had long ago stockpiled their fancy eatables and were now either fighting Gerald for some vino, or were at home with their feet in front of the fireplace channel on Netflix, and ordering delivery online. Meredith was never one to buy supplies early. She was of the opinion that if you bought eggs and milk, you were going to want a rib roast when hunkered down. Why bother buying till you knew what you were craving? After all, a last minute pie never looked so good as when you might not see fresh food again indefinitely. A *preplanned pie* however is just calories.

She'd already found the first major ingredient: three pounds of deveined precooked shrimp. They were sitting proudly in the child seat of her cart staring up at her with great enthusiasm, as if to say, *I'm going to make you sooooo happy.* She knew the SuperMarkt had lobster, so that was no problem, and she had already passed scallops on the way in, so those would quickly join her cart. The meat would always be easy on this journey; this was a German grocery store after all. The next item she required was evading her but she figured she'd find all the small easy stuff and come back for the last one.

"Is there anything we can help you find today?" A petite woman of fifty appeared behind Meredith like a sneaky Deutsch Leprechaun and stared at her with a patient smile behind some of the thickest lenses anyone's seen since they were outfitting the Hubble Telescope. Her hair resembled a skinned Ewok."Ahhh!... Oh hi. You startled me."

"So sorry about that!"

"Yes, you can actually. I need the spice section, please."

"Right this way!" The unnamed petite woman, we'll call her Betsy, led Meredith through the labyrinth of exotic and organic rices and veggies, through the aisle with fourteen different gluten free types of Molasses, and passed the velvet roped counter where the strawberries are so delicate that once you touch them you need to eat them within thirty minutes or they will shrivel into dust. Finally at the opposite end of the store, and adjacent to the Paleo-friendly dog food, the spice section almost glowed with possibility.

"Wow," Meredith whispered to herself.

"Wowwy, zowwy! Can I help you find anything else, sweetie?"

"Yeah maybe, let me look here first. Thanks."

"Surely!" and like that, she was gone. The spice section was so far in the corner, Meredith could no longer hear people, just the gentle rumble of the raw vegan baby food refrigerator. She took the spices in with her eyes and tasted each in a dish in her mind. It was a meditative feeling. She could feel the angst trickling out of her, and her shoulders relax.

"Hey babe!" Gerald appeared behind her tapping her on the shoulder with his soggy hand. She screamed and dropped a glass bottle of red salt mined from the cave next to the famous Chilean Miner cave accident.

"DAMMIT! What's wrong with you!? Who said it was okay to do that?"

"Sorry I just... I found the Chateau Clouseau!"

"Screw your Clouseau." She batted the bottle bag out of his hand, and it fell with a clunk into the cart. Fortunately the bottles were hearty and it sounded worse than it was.

"Baby. I know you're stressed, but that was the last six bottles of this stuff they're getting this week. Please use more caution when taking out your frustration." He desperately tried to contain his anger.

"You scared me."

"Sorry."

"Help me look." The two got to work scanning the hundreds of spices from top to bottom and bottom to top—one from each side to the other. They met in the middle, and switched till the whole counter was scanned twice.

"Did you see it?" she asked longingly.

"No. You?" he reciprocated.

"If I saw it, would I have asked you?" Gerald ignored her. This was not the time to start a fight. There were about fifteen minutes till those sneaky little German gnome people announced they'd need us to come to the front with our carts. *We can scream at each other at home.*

"I'll go find someone." Gerald offered. She didn't say anything and began scanning again from the top.

*****

He wandered through several aisles before he found that he had gotten himself all turned around. This place was massive. Before it became a luxury market, it was an old warehouse from the meatpacking era of NYC. A billion swine were packed and shipped from this very factory before the health department shut it down. Or so Gerald read online. It's hard to tell for sure. Though they did have black and white photos, so he knew it was at least a factory once. And whether that statistic about swine was true, it was massive regardless. He ambled among several tall shelves and found himself accidentally on the second floor cart escalator, and being a clumsy person, he decided against running upstream down the ramp, so he rode to floor two.

It was darker on this floor, and colder too. He was still sopping wet from the earlier blast of rain before entering the wine store. As he searched for the downward bound escalator, he came upon a single booth in the middle of a clearing of sorts, and in it stood one woman with an old-timey German hat, which resembled those worn in ice cream shops. There seemed to be a halo of light surrounding her booth, and a large pile of sausage cut into bite-sized chunks harpooned with toothpicks.

"Guten Abend, mein freund! Willkommen to ze SuperMarkt. Vood you care to try ein bite of our vorld famous venison sausage? I promise you'll be filled with delight!"

"Uhhh yeah, sure."

He took a chunk from the woman and looked around. "Can you direct me to... oh my God, this is delicious!" He interrupted his own question to taste.

"How do you make it so flavorful?"

"Zat is ze SuperMarkt Secret Recipe... but ve do sell zis in ze refrigerators on ze serd floor, should you like some more."

"Yeah, definitely! How do I..."

"Ze escalator is behind you."

He turned and sure enough, as though by magic, the escalator materialized.

"Thanks! This sure is tasty!"

"Glad you like it! And if you like that, don't miss ze desserts on ze fourth floor!"

"Wow! Great! Hey just a quick question. This place is closing soon, and my wife and I are trying to make..."

"Don't vorry, once you're inside, we von't close until you're ready. New policy by ze manager for ze storm."

"Oh great! She'll be thrilled to hear."

"Go on now, freund. Much left to see!"

*****

Meredith was growing worried that her idiot husband had locked himself in a walk-in freezer and began exploring the aisles to find him. She couldn't find her spices, and wasn't too thrilled, but knew that if she found her husband, at least she could send him out to a Duane Reade or some such place to look again after they were home. She had found the most important stuff already.

She moseyed down the back aisle and looked at the fresh meats again. It was very strange how few customers remained in the store—usually she had to step over a number of toddlers to get her essentials. In recent years this neighborhood had a large influx of wealthy young professionals, many of whom had babies just to dress them up or keep up with the Joneses. Schools were built. Rumors told that urban art installations would be torn down for more suburban fare. It was a haven within the city. But today, there were no infants, no puppies barking at their masters, barely any employees for goodness sakes. It was eerily quiet. So she stopped.

"Gerald!" she called out, hoping he'd hear her from behind one of the shelves and come running, but... nothing. "Gerald?" Again, no answer. She pulled out her phone and tried to ring him, but there were no bars in the back of the store here. She heard it used to be a giant military compound where the Navy planned its assaults on the Japanese and Koreans before it was decommissioned and turned into this luxury goods store. But she had read that on a Swapplē Juice Lid—their trivia is hit or miss. But it was big, and the signal did suck.

It was then, that Meredith saw a light coming through a porthole in a door in the opposite far back corner, and thought, "I've never seen that before…"

She left her cart and bee-lined to the porthole, just to sneak a peak. Tucking her face to the glass, she noticed the door led into the kitchen adjacent to the fishmonger, and though the kitchen was vacant, another red light spouted from up a small flight of stares by the sinks. She looked around carefully and wandered into the kitchen.

Stepping with the grace of a seductive deer, she calculated her every movement and glanced up the stairs. The red light was coming through an identical porthole at the top. She quickly climbed the steps and spied through this window, and a creepy sight laid just beyond the door. A long… we'll call it a hallway, but really it looked like a Greenpoint railroad apartment if it were transplanted into a submarine. The red light was coming from a large industrial orb (almost like a three dimensional Hal 9000) next to the closest door, but there were a dozen or more orbs next to a dozen or more doors stretching way back into this "hallway."

Well, Meredith never did anything halfway, so she took a deep breath and swung open the door and stood with the bravado of a western gunslinger, waiting for a monster or even just a salty custodian to jump out and tackle her. But there was no one… so she pressed onward. If someone did come along, at least she used to be an active Cross Country runner back before she met Gerald… They used to be so cute in love back then…

*****

Gerald carried three or four packages of the venison sausage tightly under his arm. He wanted to get more, but in the event the storm went rogue, he didn't want to have to throw them out when the fridge died. Now he knew where to find them, so twelve sausages would hold him for the time being.

"Now where's the fourth floor escalator..." he mumbled to himself. And as if by magic, it appeared beside him. *I need to come here more often, this place is crazy convenient!* He stepped onto the moving ramp and let it carry him upward to God knew where. Dessert, if that old lady wasn't lying. He tried to remember his old German classes to recall what "German dessert" consisted of. Was it mostly fruit based? Was it fried? Was it just cheese on stuff? It had been years. He decided to let the selection surprise him rather than think too hard about it. As he rode, he heard soft polka music from somewhere. It seemed to be getting louder as he rode, so he inferred it was on the fourth floor. It occurred to him that he hadn't spoken to his wife since he volunteered to find assistance, and checked his phone to see if she called. *Nope, guess not!* The phone beeped off—"Battery Critically Low, Please Recharge Soon"—but he didn't see the warning before he tucked it back into his pant pocket.

He arrived on the fourth floor. And lo and behold, there was dessert! Desserts of all kinds! Candy, salty treats, sweets, cupcakes, Bavarian cream filled pastries and meats, schnitzel-covered pies, whip creamed schnitzel, even two or three different insect gummies. It was a smorgasbord of delight. It was still unsettling that no one else was shopping; just Gerald and his wife... and then the live polka band that took up a corner of the floor came into focus. The stage they stood upon protruded out in a classic proscenium, and the band members marched up and back in traditional and stereotypical lederhosen. There were five of them in total: four of whom could have worked on the side for the circus as they were muscled and tight, and the fifth was a portly and mustachioed man whose socks were held up with a garter. He also wore a girdle to hold back his gut, but its days were numbered as it was only a simple girdle; the belt equivalent of a levee in New Orleans.

As the band played and marched, Gerald helped himself to a clear baggie and began filling it with various snackables. Soon the girdled mustache rose to his feet, as he had been keeping the beat with his toe from atop a wooden box drum. The other gymnast-looking musicians retreated to the back of the stage and the lights dimmed in the store. A spotlight hit him when he arrived on his mark. All was silent. Gerald stopped gorging and piling his treats and looked up. The Mustachio counted under his breath, "eins, zwei, eins zwei drei vier!" and the band erupted into the most passionate rendition of the *Tanzenade Finger Polka* the world has likely seen, and the Mustachio busted the hardest polka moves he could, quickly working up a sweat. He turned to his compatriots and grabbed a microphone on a stand and turned back to the store and began free styling lyrics in German. Gerald placed his ten bags of snacks on the ground and clapped along with giddy amusement. He whistled in approval. *Meredith would love this! Where the hell is she anyway?*

*****

At that exact moment, Meredith found herself in a cold, monotonous, and well-lit concrete hallway without further portholes to maintain her interest. She tried to double back, but each direction she turned down led to a series of continued confusion, zagging and zigging in alternatively discombobulating fashion. Her sense of forward and backward was totally out of whack and she couldn't decipher an exit. Likely she had walked into the service tunnels from when the factory used to get deliveries back in the day, though they didn't appear to be well kept or even well remembered; abandoned like yesterday's pop star.

She stopped in her tracks and checked her phone. Still no signal. In fact, less than before. She nibbled her lip and pondered her options. Glancing down at her rose gold timepiece, she ascertained that it had been at least twenty minutes since she walked away from her cart and even longer since she saw her husband. The store was about to close and she was lost in its labyrinthine bowels. The hallway offered no clear sign of escape. But she was determined and skilled beyond what one might expect, and so she swiftly placed her ear to the concrete floor below her feet and shut her eyes. It was cold and smelled earthy, but she put it out of her mind and listened. The rumbling of the industrial air conditioners became background noise and a subtle hint of a trombone radiated through the stone. She took a dozen steps each direction and repeated this process, and determined that her escape depended on that polka music not stopping at closing time. She chased that trombone vibration like her life depended on it.

*****

Not wanting to be rude, Gerald continued clapping for the Mustachio, whose solo was ramping up. He knew his wife would murder him for taking forever, but this man had no audience besides him. If a girdled mustache played his polka heart out in the forest and there was no one there to hear it... what the hell good is a polka band in the forest anyway? This struck him. *Why are they here? Why would they play when no one is shopping? Don't they have families?*

He gathered his baggies up and noticed that a number of their contents had already begun melting onto themselves and congealing in a nasty pile of cream and bacon. Using his foot, he pushed them between the barrels where the desserts were presented, and took a seat in the front row of the multiple rowed mini concert seating. The Mustachio wailed and wailed, now directing his attention to Gerald alone. Their souls seemed to hold hands at that moment, and Gerald clapped right along, knowing that when this song ended he needed to go find his wife.

*****

Meredith had already followed the trombone vibrations up two flights of stairs and through another concrete maze. The music was about to climax; she didn't have much time left... when she saw the red light emanating from a porthole at the end of the longest hallway so far. Her heart burst with joy and she bolted down the expanse, swinging the doors open like a pack of ER doctors with a gunshot patient. At last she saw a kitchen and ran through the entrance into the fourth floor of the SuperMarkt to find her husband literally holding the hand of the German

Chef Boyardi as a rambunctious polka troop climaxed on stage. All was silent except for Meredith catching her breath.

Gerald looked over and saw her panting. "Meredith! You found me!"

"Why are you holding that man's hand?" she asked between gasps.

Gerald turned back to the Mustachio and bowed to him, shaking his hand heartily. "You, sir, are a legend. I underestimated you earlier. I will tell everyone about this night."

The Mustachio said nothing, only bowed himself. And the band cleared off of the stage and the stage lights went black. The overhead store lights clicked back on and they were gone, leaving just Meredith and Gerald alone on the fourth floor, surrounded by desserts of all kinds, and about twelve venison sausages.

"Did you find everything?" Gerald asked with a look of euphoria on his face, his eyes sagging from the stimulation.

Not wanting to admit that she wandered into the depths of the factory and barely escaped, she took a moment to catch her breath fully and then said, "Mostly. Just missing the saffron."

He had forgotten entirely that he had originally walked away from his wife to find a store rep to help him find just that. His brain clicked back on and he asserted, "Well, there's no time to lose then!"

He picked up his venison and grabbed her arm and hurried around the floor trying to find the down escalator.

"Where's the..." she began.

"Oh it's nearby! This place is super convenient. The escalator must be right... HERE!" He dragged her past an aisle expecting it to appear as the *up* ones had before. But there was nothing. He whispered to himself, trying to invoke the same magic from earlier, "Now where's the third floor escalator..." but nope. "Now where's the fourth floor escalator..." Still nothing. Meredith was growing impatient.

"You know I left my cart downstairs to come find you. The meats are probably thawing."

"The escalators can handle carts, why didn't you bring it with you when you came up?" Gerald asked, mystified that she wasn't nearly as ecstatic about the store as he was.

"Escalators?"

"How did you find me then?"

"I took the stairs."

"There are stairs here?"

The two stopped and looked at each other in confusion, then pressed on, ignoring that last conversation when they passed an elevator.

"Wait, Gerald, back there!" She pointed to it, with all its vertical transportive glory.

"Great!" he said, and they went straight for it.

It arrived in a jiffy and they were quickly whisked down to the main floor. They rounded a few aisles where they were greeted by the mole people that ran the store. They were not thrilled with their customers. Gerald and Meredith were embarrassed by this confrontation.

"You know the store was supposed to close thirty minutes ago? We can't lock up till you are gone."

"We are sooo sorry!" Gerald began.

"Yes, immensely sorry! It was a total fluke, we got a little lost looking for an item, and lost track of time!" Meredith finished.

"If you can help us find some saffron and our cart, we can check right out of here!"

"Firstly, your cart has been emptied back into wherefrom you pulled the items. You left it almost an hour ago. Secondly, that's a specialty item, and it is most commonly used in Spanish Paellas..."

"Yes exactly! We're making paella for our friends because of the storm! We're calling it Hurricane Paella, and we're making Hurricane drinks, it's going to be great fun!" Gerald rattled on.

"Let me finish, please," the leprechaun woman stated seriously. "It is most commonly used in *SPANISH* Paellas, so why would you try to find a specialty *SPANISH* item at our *GERMAN* SuperMarkt? It's kinda crazy to think about. Would you go searching for lemongrass at a Brazilian Butcher shop?"

"I don't know what lemongrass is," Gerald said frowning.

"So, you have no saffron, and you emptied our cart onto the shelves..."

"You've outstayed your welcome, we need to lock up, my children have already called three times crying that they were scared of the thunder."

"It is not my concern whether your children were pooping themselves in a Museum. I came to this store because you are an exotic goods shop and you should sell everything, especially as your spice section is plentiful."

"Exotic? We're German, that's hardly exotic. We have meats and veggies and some treats and that's the way of it."

"Some? You have oodles," Gerald interjected, sensing the growing hostility. "Your fourth floor is overflowing with different weird and exotic treats...

also you have a badass polka band by the way, can I get their name? I want to look them up."

"This conversation is over. We don't have saffron, we don't have a fourth floor, we don't even have a second floor. Georg, will you show these people out please?"

"No second floor?!" Meredith interrupted again. "Don't try to insult my intelligence, this place is cavernous and full of strange lights and my husband was holding some fat polka guy's hand!"

"If you found a way upstairs, then you trespassed on some other tenants property and got physical with said tenant, because we are just a one-story German supply shop. Georg, please?"

Georg, the only tall employee at the store, grabbed the couple by their wrists and dragged them to the front, pushing them through the automatic doors and onto the curb, which was still being pelted by Sandy's monsoon. The doors were locked behind them and the lights snuffed out.

Gerald and Meredith stood shell-shocked by the weirdness that just befell them. "At least you got the wine... the... what's it called... The Chateau Clouseau."

"You knocked it into the cart when I found you by the spices," he said almost in a trance.

Meredith turned to him, numb, and said nothing for a long time. The two moseyed to the valet stand, which had long been abandoned by the drivers. Their car was parked out front with the driver's side window down, with the keys under a windshield wiper, and three parking tickets to boot. They got into the car that had filled with about three or four inches of rain.

"We told them we'd make a paella, and we'd have wine and Hurricanes."

"Yes, we did."

"This is the worst thing ever. We'll never be able to show our faces at the yacht club again."

"No, we won't."

"Our social lives are over."

"...Yes. Yes, they are."

Gerald turned on the car. Though it took a minute of key turning, the engine roared to life and the radio came on. *Tanzenade Finger Polka* was playing. Gerald looked up through the windshield at the SuperMarkt, and alas, on the fourth floor at the window stood the girdled mustache holding a candelabra looking down at them. One moment later, the Mustachio blew out the candles and he was gone from sight.

"Jeeves," Gerald held down his smartphone's home button. "What song is this?"

"Listening!" the robot voice said, and began scanning the sounds of the polka. *At least there will be one bit of closure to this evening.*

"I'm sorry about this, Gerald, but I don't know this song." The phone went silent. The song ended.

"This is the end of the world."

"Harrison's Interesting Adventure"

Morning, December 21, 2012 — Bucktown, Chicago

It was a beautiful morning. The birds were chirping. The flowers were sprawled out tanning. Bugs of all kinds were out creating weekend-esque traffic jams trying to get in and out of popular floral pastures. Man, was it nice. It was a Friday, but it really felt like a Saturday, as there wasn't a care in the world for anyone around. For one yuppie man, freelance no doubt, this perfection was irrelevant to him.

Every day was the same, as he worked whenever he wanted, and that happened to be every day. He was an avid blogger. He wrote volumes on ways to improve your cat's mood, and how to make a backyard grill pit using just the items in your garage. This was ironic because as it happened, he lived in Bucktown, Chicago and his apartment complex didn't have a garage. He had a space in a garage nearby reserved for his Prius, but he paid out the tailpipe for it. He had arranged everything in his life, "just so." Divergence from the formula was bad for productivity and creativity, he found. Have you ever, for example, tried a new Chinese restaurant and then written an overture? Exactly, no one writes his or her opus when being spontaneous. It's a rookie mistake. Not that he could write music anyway, but he certainly listened to it.

"Harken Stone??" asked the same barista who *always* made his drink every morning for over a year.

"That's *Harrison*," he replied as he snatched the iced drink away.

"Have a good day, Harrison, come back again."
The barista smiled. This was her favorite part of the day. Anyone who has that many idiosyncrasies about his or her coffee needs to get a real job. He never spoke to her about his job, but something about him screamed blogger. Maybe his Felix sweater, or his messenger bag. He sure as hell wasn't a messenger with *those* legs.

"You too, Shasta," he responded trying to be cute.

"Racism never looked good on nobody, Harry."

"Racism? I'm not a..." He took a closer look at her nametag.

"Cindy? You're a Cindy?"

"See? What'd I say?"

"It really looked like Shasta or something exotic. I swear, I didn't know!"

"Get out, boy, don't make it worse. See you tomorrow."

She pulled out a neon pink drink, "March-of-dimes?"

"Marigold?" whispered a frail old lady who could barely see over the counter.

"Have a good day, Marigold, come back again."

Harrison, sufficiently butt-hurt, hobbled out of the Starbucks and onto Damen Avenue. He'd never been so insulted in his life. Literally. He went to the best schools (his affluent parents saw to that), had the best teachers, and had recommendations that got him internships under chairmen at NASA.

I've earned my success, what do you know 'Cindy?' I don't even believe that's your name. I'm going to write a letter to the manager. He pondered which of his six varieties of stationary he wanted to use, when out of the sky a blast of light shot down and saturated the very air in front of him. He fell to his knees and covered his face, screaming.

"Harrison?" He started to roll on the ground thinking he'd been struck by lightning and was in shock.

"Harrison?" His screaming only intensified. *Holy crap holy crap holy crap holy crap....*

"HARRISON!" the light reached over and tapped him a bit too roughly on the shoulder. He stopped screaming and looked up to see this floating ball of light staring at him.

"Good morning, Harrison."

"Good morning." He didn't know what to make of this.

"Harrison, I am God," the face clarified, as *this dude* was obviously taken unaware. The ball of light spun around like dye in a bucket of water until it formed a floating face with a white nicely trimmed beard and a crown of gold.

"God? Like *the* God?" Harrison asked in utter confusion.

"Are there any others?"

"Yeah: Buddha, Vishnu, Allah, Ra..."

"Real gods!" the giant face bellowed, offended at the implication.

"Alrighty then." Harrison sipped his coffee.

"Listen, Harrison, I need your help."

"What? Do you want me to be a prophet or a martyr? Or maybe lead an exodus? Ya know, I hear slavery's still around..." Harrison wasn't the most eloquent when confronted directly.

"No, Harrison. What I need is not in your ability to lead, or in your skills as a prophet. What I need is something... a little more... physical."

"What does that mean?!" Harrison covered up his nips with his slender arms.

"That means I'm having Moses speak at an anti-drug conference in Toledo. And he has a bit of a problem with narcolepsy."

"Like the sleeping disorder?"

"THE VERY SAME!!"

"And what do you want from me?" A chorus of angels picked up their lyres that were on the floor of the cloud they were sitting on, and simultaneously broke into an ominous and yet familiar song. The floating face shape shifted into an arrow and pointed itself at his right hand, cradling the sacred beverage.

"Whoa dude! You want my coffee!!?"

"Yes. Can I please have it?" The arrow transformed into a hand and signaled to the chorus to back off a little. The angel conductor softened his conducting and smiled. The arrow of light reverted to the floating face and looked at Harrison with pleading eyes.

"Why? You're God, you can make your own! Or buy one or something!"

"See the thing about that is... I got behind in my taxes and now to make up for it, the federal government takes away all my tithings for reimbursement. And about the making it thing... the leading stockholder in Starbucks Inc. is actually Lucifer. And he's a little sue-happy if you know what I mean. So you see my problem."

Feeling a little overwhelmed, Harrison rubbed his free hand through his fantastically conditioned hair. "...The almighty God wants my coffee... there are thousands of other people drinking coffee, and he chooses to harass me..."

"HARASS!? I am the Lord of Hosts!"

"What kinda host doesn't have a plan for coffee?"

"There's more than one kind of Host," God rebutted, growing a little cranky.

"Why can't you just go get a cheap one or something?" Harrison whined.

God sighed. "Moses won't do the conference with just *any* coffee; it's gotta be from Starbucks. Celebrities are very particular."

"But why me??" Harrison was overwhelmed and confused, and slightly cold and clammy.

"Alright, to sweeten the deal, Hare..." The floating face transformed into a whole bodied but archaically dressed man, and sat down on the curb next to him. He patted the pavement, inviting Harrison to sit next to him. "I will offer you what I did Solomon: what is the one thing you want more than anything else in the world right now?"

"Evidently the one thing you want more than anything else right now..."

"Oh come on now! What about Wisdom? Or complete and utter inner peace?"

"Ehhhh. Google has made it so you don't really need wisdom in this world. All you need are guns and scapegoats, and you'll be fine."

God was growing desperate. "Do you want those?"

"I've got one of each, thanks," Harrison opened his jacket and revealed his antique pistol in a shoddy leather holster he bought in Cairo on the vacation he took with his parents as his eighth grade graduation present.

"How'd you manage a carry permit in Chicago?"

"Connections. My family knows a guy or two."

"I'm shocked, a white privileged fellow like you?" God said sarcastically as he rubbed his neck. It didn't really bother Harrison, he'd heard it all before. He chocked it up to jealousy. God considered his options for a bit of time.

"Look, I'll be right back..." The cherubim sang their mighty song, and the lightning struck upwards to the sky, only to re-strike the ground a moment later.

"Okay, I talked the situation over with Moses, and he will be flexible. He will take a different drink." The chorus of angels sang a joyous song in a hundred octaves.

"But! It has to have a large amount of caffeine... and it must be tasty. What do you suggest?"

"What about that Red Weasel Energy Nectar, I hear that one's pretty good? Or some... guarana-heavy concoction that the kids drink these days... what's it called... Pulque?"

"A'ight, I'll be back in one sec." Once again God disappeared in a flash, and the choirs sang, prompting a slight ringing in Harrison's ears. His mother always told him someday he'd meet God, but he never figured it'd be in front of a juice bar. He longed to escape from this terrible distraction. He started compiling in his mind a list of places to eat for the summer he could post about. Just thinking about the search engine optimization on this list-to-be soothed his nerves. But sure enough, the man of light reappeared in front of him.

"Alright look, I've surveyed the territory of energy drinks and decided that Starbucks is the only way. Red Weasel is just the nasty cancer-y aftertaste without the caffeine, and Pulque is just a nasty milky drink from Aztec days... so neither will do the trick. So I'm gonna need your bevvy please."

"Not gonna happen, bub." Harrison sipped his iced coffee, which was starting to melt from all the supernatural surges of energy occurring in front of him. Harrison's face was also a mite toasty from the radiation, and wiped a little of the condensation from his cup on his face to cool off, but this suggestive gesture angered God. This delay was beginning to make him more desperate as well: Moses didn't ask for half a coffee, he asked for a whole coffee. Even if he could break Harrison's fortitude, this was becoming a lost cause with each sip.

"....What if you talked to Satan for me? I'll get you his number. Maybe you can do some of his bidding in exchange..."

"Why don't you just get a job there?" Harrison suggested brashly.

"'CAUSE I HAVE NO BODY! Wait a minute! I have a brilliant idea: I could send Jesus back! Since he does have a body, he could work there! Getting me free coffee!!" The chorus erupted in song, and several seraphim took selfies of themselves with God and Harrison in the background.

"Wouldn't that equate to the Second Coming of Christ or something?" Harrison asked losing patience.

"I guess. Depending on your lawyer. But we can let the National Enquirer have this one... And if it scores me free stuff, maybe it's about time for a comeback!" The most hardcore looking angel picked up an electric guitar and played a killer solo.

"I hear Starbucks has good benefits, too."

"Yeah, I've heard of that. All right, well thank you, sir. When the rapture comes, I'll go easy on you for your help." God's glowing cloud-body spun around and transformed again into a solid ball of light and slid upwards towards the heavens and the choirs sang a soft hymnal to play him off the earthly stage.

Harrison stood there on the street, paralyzed for a long while, but decided this strange episode was the result of sleep deprivation and proceeded to hurry away. He chugged a big gulp of his artisanal-style flavored iced coffee and ducked into an L station to get underground, just in case the light ball came back. He walked to the center of the platform, knowing he'd never get on a train by the stairs. He spent the following 27 minutes in shock and awe, slowly and carefully pondering why the hell he just hallucinated so intensely.

Could it be the organic zucchini bread he'd been eating for the last few months? Or was this a sign of a bigger problem: did the glyphosate-covered GMO processed foods of yesteryear cross his blood-brain barrier and this was the first symptom of a Monsanto-induced tumor rearing its ugly head in the form of organized religion? He was unsure. Since it came on rapidly and disappeared just as rapidly, perhaps it was just a fleeting moment of insanity. Perhaps he was due for a trip to his artisanal general practitioner for some aromatherapy and eastern chanting. *Yes, the doctor is the solution!* And fortunately, the doc was right off of the blue line as well. He didn't need to re-route, which was the first step towards him getting back to his regular routine.

The train lights cut through the darkness of the tunnel and he could feel his blood pressure regulating. As the train settled into the station he whispered some words his guru taught him to calm his breathing. When the door opened, a man in a brilliantly tailored Tom Ford suit stepped forth, wearing Rainbow sandals and sporting a rugged surfer do. He removed his aviators and his eyes met Harrison's.

"Hey, uhhh, Harrison?" asked the sexy stranger. Harrison's memory failed him as he tried to place the man in his mind. *Was it at the meet-up in Wicker Park last year? Is he an investor from a roundtable in the Loop? He really rocks those sandals...*

"Can I get a sip of your coffee?" he asked politely. Harrison realized in an instant who it was and his heart rate instantly shot up. He was speechless, but the man knew what to do. He raised his hand, and by the force of the heavens, Harrison's coffee lifted from his hand and floated through the air to the man's perfectly tanned fingers. Jesus made a pistol of his hand and divinely blasted the drink before he took a gulp from it.

"Sweet *Gautama* Mama, that hits the spot!" He snapped his almost-feminine fingers, teleporting the vessel back into Harrison's quivering grip. Harrison was shocked and confused and amazed. He pulled the coffee to his lips and took a little on his tongue before spitting it out on the platform.

133

"Jesus! You spiked my coffee!"

"Oh right, sorry." Jesus made another pistol of his hand and extracted the booze from Harrison's drink once again. "Awhile back, I used to be a bum. That's what we do. Sorry about that. But see, I got a *real* job now: serving *yuppies*."

Harrison could tell that Jesus was none too thrilled with his current assignment. Washing poor peoples' feet is one thing, but rich people... not so much. "But I tell you... as soon as Moses gets what he wants, I'm outta here. 'Cause there's nothing worse than serving yuppies."

He put on his sunglasses and walked from the platform, and with his departure, so too did the train depart, leaving Harrison to catch the next one. As Jesus ascended from the station, he came upon a man blocking the stairwell on his phone talking loudly to a loved one or at least his mistress. "No, I love you more... no, I love you more... no, you!" Jesus threw up his hands in annoyance and made a pistol of his hand, celestially zapping him from the top of the stairs to God knows where. He entered the Chicago air en route to his first day of work.

*****

That night as Harrison lie in his bed wearing his favorite flannel pajamas, to his dismay a breaking news story interrupted his regularly scheduled programming. The news anchor appeared on screen with a worried look on his face.

"This is Robert Warner with Channel Four News. There was a disturbance in progress just a few minutes ago at the local Starbucks by a man only identifiable via his name tag, 'Jesus.' Take a look at the tape, but be warned it can be disturbing to younger viewers."

The feed cut to a security camera over the counter of the Starbucks where Harrison buys his gourmet beverages every morning. Sitting at a small table in the corner were two preppy teen girls awaiting their orders.

"So I was like, mom, if you're going to buy me a new pair of UGGs, at least... don't buy me... the mint green ones? Get the beige ones or at the very least the lavender ones for Christsakes. Who does she think she is? And I'm only asking for like two or three pairs—I need them to get through the season..."

Harrison sat up, immediately recognizing the man from the train platform.

"Green Tea Lattes." He slammed the drinks on the table in front of the teens.

The girl expounding on her traumatic experience with her mother turned to him with utter disdain and spoke slowly.

"Well, Hey-Zus... we ordered peppermint hot chocolates. PEPPERMINT HOT CHOCOLATES," she turned to her friend, "you think he speaks English?" before turning back to Jesus. "HOT. CH... No, wrong, wrongo drinko, no!"

"Si..." replied Jesus, trying to hold his tongue. He picked up the overpriced drinks and walked to make them hot chocolates instead, when the girl said under her breath, "Jesus Christ, these people can't do anything right..." This struck a nerve for Jesus, as he had done a ton of charity work with the downtrodden in a former life.

"That's it!" He turned back to the girl and grabbed her arm, dragging her from the table. "Out! Get out!"

"Excuse... Me..." she uttered while he removed her. "Are you getting me another drink?"

"MOVE!"

The other girl could only sit and watch as the employee tossed her friend out of the store. The friend snapped to her senses and rose to her feet, "Oh my God!!" She ran to the door, and pulled out her phone to videotape the exchange when Jesus pulled her outside. The security feed kept rolling a long moment and in the background the women seemed to disappear without a trace. Jesus finally returned to the store, removing his apron and tossing it on the floor.

He sighed loudly and walked behind the counter and poured a hot coffee in a travel cup and put a lid on it. His face became zen and he raised his hand to the heavens. To no avail. After a moment of nothing, he opened his eyes looking around before looking back up at the ceiling.

"Beam me up, Scotty!" he snarled. And with that, Jesus disappeared from the shop in a burst of light.

And in time with the television, a loud explosion sounded from outside Harrison's window. Harrison was startled and crawled across his bed to look for the cause of the ruckus. In the distance and closing in, the cloud of debris and radiation was coming his way from a centrally located mushroom cloud. He stared in horror. *The Second Coming is true!* His phone dinged, and he looked down to see a notification from the furniture import shop he had logged into the day before.

"Your order has shipped. Your package should arrive in two to three days." He turned to face his apartment. *And I never got that alligator skin ottoman!*

And on December 21, 2012, at 9:00 pm, all was silent.

"Pearl Harbor 2: Pearl Harborer!"

0500 Hours Honolulu Time,
December 21, 2012 — Pearl Harbor

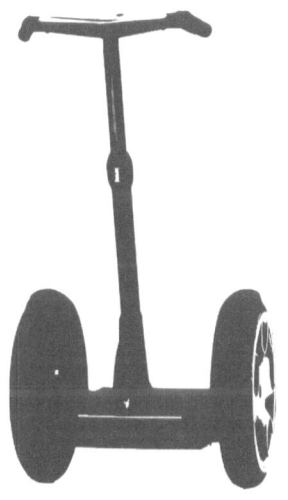

"**M**aggots!"

The usual unpleasant ring of his phone stirred Cliff Kōno from his sleep. "Maggots!...Maggots!... Maggots!..." He smacked the snooze, and rolled back over trying to forget what today was... or rather, what day was it anyway?

Every day was pretty much identical: every morning had the same routines, every afternoon had duplicate duties, every night was filled with drunken debauchery trying to forget what today was, and what tomorrow will inevitably be again.

Kōno was a young man. Not the youngest on the sub, but far from the oldest. He had enlisted after years and years of family squabbles left him longing to flee from their home in the middle of the night like a bandit in a French novel some seven years before.

Cliff fancied himself an artist, born to a doctor and a scientist. His sisters were training to be a physicist and a pharmacist. His cousins? Engineers and physicians. Lab techs and pharmacologists. Medical examiners and... well, you get it.

Kōno wrote poetry about femme fatales and noir-ish places, people with a gun in each sleeve and a boot-knife to boot. He was interested in the inner lives of characters, not the external sores of cranky old ones. His parents felt betrayed that he wasn't pursuing their interests so they shunned him, and his siblings abandoned him for fear of reprisal.

The Navy seemed like the way out. Or at least a way to make money halfway across the pacific, where no backseat driver family members could belittle him or his dreams. And have you seen their commercials? I mean, wow! They are pretty epic. They make you feel like you could be Clint MacCloud from those popular action movies, "Live Tough" and the critically acclaimed sequel, "Live Tougher: Tough Life." What's not to love?

So he fled. Now this may seem like an impulsive move for an educated guy, but every day at home added another nail in the coffin. From his youngest years, he was always *lesser than* compared to his sisters—he was never the smart one, nor the pretty one, never the ambitious one, nor the determined one. He loved life. Just most times it didn't really love him back the way he'd like. His parents reminded him of how grateful he should be every day. And maybe they were right—he had a roof over his head and food in his belly. But so do murderers in cellblock C.

He packed a daypack duffle with a few pairs of clothes, a roll of Oreos, and his favorite comics, and moseyed to the bus in the center of his small suburban town outside of the Twin Cities, and waited. He pulled out a small bouncy ball from his pocket and threw it against the courthouse adjacent to the bus stop. It was early so no one would be in for a few hours. The morning air felt cold, more so than he was prepared for and after a few minutes of breathing icy wind into his lungs, he knew he'd need to make a stop.

He keyed back into his house and dug out his winter coat from the closet under the stairs, when he heard the floorboards creak. The upstairs light turned on. The dancing Mickey on his wrist made it clear that no one should be up for another hour!

His mother's silhouette appeared on the wall next to the front door and he knew he was done for, his freedom was not to be, he'd be a Doctor, or possibly even a male nurse, and nothing was more humiliating to him than Mursedom. He closed his eyes and squatted down next to the closet. A slender stream squeezed from his ducts, and he sniffled, wiping away the tears with his left hand.

Creak. Creak. Creak. She methodically hit every step with all her weight. Creak. He crossed his arms over his legs and sighed out deeply. Defeated. Sad. Alone, in a house with his family. Miles away from his closest friends. Creak. Creak Creak. Creak. She stepped onto the landing. Creak creak creak. Now all was lost. She stumbled towards the kitchen with the finesse of an obese German shepherd, bumping into the coat rack and the ottoman in the living room.

She opened the fridge in the kitchen and her face lit up in the evening light, but something was off. Cliff looked at her and realized he wasn't done for at all! She was sleepwalking! He jumped to his feet and tip toed to the front door across the beige might-as-well-be-shag carpet that he loathed so much. Stepping onto the hardwood in the foyer, a familiar creak erupted and echoed off the high walls and his slumbering mum spun around like the Cyclops to Odysseus.

He opened the door and ran out, slamming the door a little too hard for comfort behind him, and she stomped to the door behind him, but simply locked the door and nothing more was heard. He was back in the cold air under a full moon, and trace snowflakes had begun falling daintily around him like little fairies and princesses. He took in this moment, for it could be his last time home.

He breathed in deep the frigid air, and sighed out his worries. Everything was going to be okay. He was joining the Navy. He boarded the bus on Main Street, which took him about forty minutes south to the enlistment center.

It was dark and the recruiters wouldn't be in till about eight or so, so he pulled out his ball and once again bounced it on the ground and off the bricks near the bus stop. It was amazing the difference in his mood before the sun came up to now. He played with his ball till he saw a man dressed in full uniform and followed him into the recruiter's office.

Fast forward two days. Cliff landed in Hawaii with dozens of other young hopefuls and was ushered onto a Navy bus with bright exciting graphics plastered on the side, though the inside left much to be desired as it turned out to be a rather old and stagnant bus. It smelled like someone's nerves got the best of them in one way or another.

The recruits took their seats and waited in silence for the uniformed officer to speak. He double-checked his clipboard and then triple-checked and quadruple-checked before introducing himself.

"Good morning, Maggots. I am Chief Petty Officer Braden. Welcome to the rest of your life."

*****

On the last day of human existence on Earth, or at least human existence as it has remained for the last 10,000 years or so, some events transpired. Some call it a series of coincidences. But Petty Officer Cliff Kōno didn't believe in coincidences. From experience, he was a man that felt that if you're being kicked, there has to be someone doing the kicking. So what is Armageddon if not one really pissed off and coordinated celestial group of soccer hooligans? I'll explain.

When folks discussed the *End of Days*, they usually went back and forth: "It's a zombie plague!" "No, it's the Second Coming!" "You're wrong, it's nuclear holocaust!" Well. Everyone was pretty much right. There were bombs falling, planes stalling, zombies biting, nuns fighting, pigs flying, puppies dying, and of course this was the uncanny moment when the South decided to rise again. Right alongside the dead. Who knew that the second Civil War would be between the modern south and the confederates? It was like watching a dog chase its tail. And then bite it off. Let me begin again.

On December 21, 2012, Cliff was stationed on a nuclear submarine at Pearl Harbor. They classified him as a nuclear technician, not because he was actually specialized—aside from his two-week-long seminar in the conference room—but because he attended a year of college. Many of his fellow petty officers barely went to high school. They could barely form a sentence without resorting to childish name calling. His background in the arts got him called a lot of things by almost everyone. To the recruits, Cliff was the proverbial pack of British smokes. But this was nothing new.

Now one would think that the nuclear sub element would be something to write home about, since they're gigantically expensive deadly floating military bases... but it wasn't. His Navy life consisted of asking for permission. For what? For everything. You want to go to the bathroom? Ask permission. You want to do your work for the day? Ask permission. You want to combine two tasks into one? Oh, you better believe you're asking permission. "Efficiency" and "military" are not synonymous. Ya wonder why the US Military budget's so high? Ask me permission to ask me about it and I'll tell ya.

His average day began at 0500 hours. The morning bell would go off and the petty officers would climb out of their bunks to line up, and the commanding officer in charge that day would greet everyone and tell them it was time to get to work. They'd receive their assignments. And again, let me emphasize: if the Navy was anything, it was hierarchical.

"Permission to shine the turbines?"

"Permission granted!"

"Permission to disengage from this conversation to proceed to shine the turbines?"

"Permission granted!"

"Permission to thank the commanding officer for his acceptance of this petty officer's proposal to shine the turbines?"

"Permission granted!"

"Thank you sir!"

It would go on and on like this. Okay, it wasn't that insane. But yes, that shade of Crayon is in the correct section of purples.

Remember when I mentioned the Navy recruitment commercials? You ever see 'em? Where hard rock music rips through the speakers, and determined young men and women tear through the sky in jet fighters, while aircraft carriers decimate dolphin habitats at enormous speeds? And just watching it, you can feel the thrill and excitement of the career that will make you a noble patriot and change your life forever? Cliff mopped the galley this morning. Not once. But twice! He forgot to ask permission the first time, so they made him do it again. But not before calling him a variety of slurs that

I won't share with you. Even at the *End of Days*, one must be courteous.

*****

It was an average morning. Cliff received many permissions before and after the incident, and proceeded to seek out his commanding officer to get permission to move onto sorting the lubricants in the supply hold when he heard a scream. Now you wouldn't normally hear anything like that... outside of the ship's annual "Halloscream Contest," where the underlings like Cliff and his bunkmates were grouped in either group one or two and whichever team couldn't scream the loudest pledge of allegiance was forced to assume the responsibilities of the winners (this was their idea of a fun time...).

He heard a scream coming from the main deck, so he ran up and saw a man bisected, writhing on the deck, and a bigger man with a giant reaping tool, in full black cape and hood (the cape was Gucci actually) swinging away at the other petty officers. Now he couldn't see his face, but Cliff was sure of one thing: based on the officers he was swinging at, and given what he was wearing, this guy was getting shot. Don't wear a hood around good ol' boys—Cliff can cite precedent on that one.

But this guy was no ordinary guy. When a small team of armed officers approached, and laid down a hail of hell upon him, it simply got his attention and he spun around to scythe them in half. He must've been rocking some serious PCP. Cliff's commanding officer one time told him about the insurgent Cong back in 'Nam who would get hopped up on a cocktail of crazy drugs and attack you like Walmart shoppers on Black Friday. He spoke fondly of those days, God knows why.

Anyway back to the story, the dude swung around like Gandalf in battle and the more officers that tried to intercede, the bigger he seemed to get as he cut them down. When it finally occurred to Cliff, he didn't just *seem* to be bigger, he *was* bigger: he had grown to north of twelve feet tall, pursuing these high school drop outs like a crusty dean.

After what seemed to be a lifetime of blood and guts being strewn about on deck, an act of carnage that Cliff's initial reaction was "find the commander and... get permission to begin mopping their entrails," it struck him that no one else was coming. All was quiet. The robed man shrunk back down to about 5' 7" and spun around toward him. Since Cliff wasn't combative, there was no need to strike like a panther, and the robed man suavely slid across the deck toward him. Cliff couldn't see his face, as it was sufficiently hidden behind the cloth. Cliff wondered if this was actually a monk that cracked up. But onward the robed man came until he was just in front of him. He leaned in closely and stared Cliff in the face.

"Kōno, Cliff?"

"Yessir?"

"The Kōno, Cliff that attended college in Brooklyn Center, Minnesota in the fall of 2004 through spring of 2005?"

"Yessir."

"Goooooood. Come."

The hooded figure lifted his arm and slid a silken glove over his pale hand that appeared skeletal, or at least like he had a bad case of eczema, and he grabbed Cliff's hand, dragging him to ship's edge.

"Look out there, Kōno, Cliff," the robed man gestured to the sky, "What do you see?"

"Sir?" Cliff's inflection seemed to change the subject.

"What?"

"Is there a reason you're saying my name like a phone book?"

"Kōno, Cliff, no more questions at this time. Look to the clouds on the horizon."

Cliff turned his gaze to the sky and noticed that very slowly the clouds turned from bright white to a dark gray.

"Whoa! That's the fastest I've ever seen a storm come through here!"

"You see the darkness approaching?" asked the robed man, with an ominous sadism in his voice.

"Yessir."

"Look closer, Kōno, Cliff." The robed man leaned in and pointed. The cloud tore asunder and after a short time something(s) popped out on the wind, riding the air current like a surfer.

"What am I looking at?" Cliff asked confused.

"Kōno, Cliff, do you know what day it is?"

"Is it Christmas day?" The man sighed and smacked his non-gloved hand on his... well it sorta disappeared into the hood and made a clacking noise, I guess it was a facepalm? He rolled up his sleeve and displayed his Casio watch for Cliff.

"What date is that?" pointing towards the small numbers on the top of the screen.

"The 21st."

"Right, not Christmas! Do you know what that means?"

"Of course. It's *almost* Christmas!"

"You're missing the point here, kid. Christmas is not a relevant factor here. Ya know what, let's back up, do you know who I am?"

"You look like Tom Cruise in Eyes Wide Shut."

"I'm taller than him, let's be real here."

"Then I don't know, sir." The dark figure sighed again, obviously annoyed at his choice of Witness.

"I am Death."

"Is that your rap name?"

"Rap na... RAP NAME?!"

"I was just asking."

"No it's not my rap name! I am Death! The specter of the life hereafter; he that ushers the poor souls over the threshold of darkness into the abyss! The collector of spirits, the crusher of lives! The ender of games!"

"I like that book, talk about a killer ending..."

"Kōno, Cliff, I need you to focus now. You're obviously not getting it. I'm the Grim Reaper. Not a name I fancy, it feels like a roller derby name, but maybe you understand better that way. I'm here because today I've come to collect the debt humanity owes, for today is Armageddon and all shall perish!"

"Okay, let me just say, for a guy who doesn't seem into entertainment, you sure do make a lot of references—Tom Cruise, Ender's Game, Armageddon..."

One could actually hear Mr. Reaper's eyes roll in his head. He grabbed Cliff's scalp and directed his attention to the patch of sky from before, and held it there.

"What do you see?"

"Uhhh..."

"That's right, the Four Horsemen of the Apocalypse. They're here to clean house. Do you get that?"

"Are you sure?" Cliff asked. "Something isn't quite right, if that's true."

Death was confused and turned to look at the clouds, and sure enough, Cliff did have something right: there were Three Horsemen and one man on some weird object rolling across the sky...

"Just a second." Death pulled out a phone and made a call behind his back in muffled whispers. After two minutes of back and forth, Death turned back to Cliff and admitted, "Okay, there was an accident with one of the horses on the way in. It twisted its ankle and they put it down... so today of all days.... Here comes the Three Horsemen..." Death sighed. "...And One Segwayman of the Apocalypse..."

Death was all sighs this morning. *You rehearse for 10,000 years, and the day of the recital... the one time!*

"So that's that." Death crossed his arms, annoyed at the failed theatrics.

"Doesn't really have the same ring to it, does it?" Cliff asked.

"No it doesn't. But the Segwayman is still pretty deadly even without his horse. He's trained in Krav Maga."

"I mean, it's a pretty popular martial art, I've trained in Krav Maga for goodness sake. At a mall. Can he do anything else?"

"Yes! He, uhh..." Death looked hard at them rolling across the sky. "Yeah, there you go, look he has a gun!"

"Okay." Cliff nodded politely.

"What?"

"Nothing."

"What? What is it?"

"Look, not to judge, as you're the judger of humanity and all..."

"The *judge*, not judger... bad english that's what that is."

"Yeah potato/ potahto, you're the judge of humanity, but half of the US is packing heat. If all he has is Krav Maga and a rifle, he's in for some trouble when he gets to Oklahoma and Montana. Even here, not everyone's all smiles and alohas... people like their guns is my point."

"Kōno, Cliff, I'm gonna stop you right there. I don't know what his game plan is, but suffice it to say, today has been prophesied for millennia, and it will go off without a hitch... even despite the slight previous hitch. So forget the logistics... he's still a Horseman who happens to be on a Segway, he's trained with the infantry..."

"Cavalry."

"What?"

"If he's a horseman, he'd be with the cavalry."

"Pipe. Down. Kōno. He has a badge sowed to his vest for goodness sake. So shut up and get ready. I'm here today to let you know you are the Witness!"

"Isn't everyone a witness? They can see it too." Cliff pointed at the screaming hoards of civilians running away in the distance. "Also, again, entertainment, 'Witness' was a movie about the Amish."

Death ignored Cliff's latter point. "You're gonna be around the longest. You'll write it all down, before we kill you."

"Oh I see."

"Good."

"Right."

"Yep."

They shared a moment of silence, looking at each other, sizing one another up.

"Hey Death, what's that the Horseman has on his head?" Death turned back to the Horsemen rolling across the sky.

"He's wearing a crown, it's symbolic, you see.... Oh dammit!"

And Cliff was gone. Ran off when Death wasn't looking. Death got back on his phone.

Ring ring! Ring ring!

"Hello, Famine here, who's this?"

"Firstly, a Segway?" Death screamed into the phone. "Come on, we're storming the castle on armored horseback, and you stroll up on an ostrich...is it amateur hour or what?"

"Hello Death, yes it's nice to talk to you too."

153

"Shut up. Just calling because The Witness escaped. I'll send you a photo of the kid, don't kill him when you find him."

"Okay, copy that. Also you let The Witness escape? Talk about amateur hour man!"

"One more word and I swear..." Death was seething.

"Swear what?" Famine laughed.

"Oh go practice your Krav Maga, you slack jaw. I'm hanging up."

"Typical." *Click*! The phone disconnected and Famine, AKA Horseman Number Three AKA the Segwayman, smiled.

"Boys, The Witness escaped. We gotta find him soon. Last seen in the proximity of Pearl Harbor. Spread out. We rendezvous when we get him."

*****

Cliff ran through the streets of this town that he had come to call his own, but didn't take time to give in to nostalgia as the bars, taquerias, and pizza joints he frequented burned down in the most delicious smelling holocaust presumably the world had ever experienced. His friends were scattered. He was alone in the world without a shoulder to cry on... unless you counted the numerous dead that lined the streets. He could cry on their shoulders. But that wasn't gonna help much. Also germs. He practiced his breathing he learned in Basic as he sprinted as quickly as he could. Though he didn't have an explicit plan, he did have a vague one and aimed for the Ko'olau Range northeast of Pearl Harbor. In every disaster movie he had seen, the survivors of the initial attack always hiked, ran, or rode their way to higher ground, and who knows?

There might even be a cave he could hide out in till Armageddon was over.

After clearing much of his immediate neighborhood, Cliff came to a series of on-ramps and off-ramps to the highways right near the stadium. He stopped to check his phone and catch his breath, but of course there was no signal to determine his location. The one lane road he had been jogging up was fairly exposed, but because of the elevated entrances and the trees lining the street, he couldn't see any other landmarks beyond the stadium itself. Most of his free time was spent near the base, so this was a bit out of his comfort zone.

He was fairly certain the road he was on ran north south. The only way to know for sure was compare against a compass or at least the sun, but since he forgot his compass, he had to settle for the latter. For those unaware, in order to determine direction based on the sun, one must track the direction of its shadow as it moves. Which requires about fifteen minutes of watching a stick cast a shadow on pavement. Normally this would be a tedious endeavor, but today with a flock of superhuman murderers after him, it seemed rather implausible. However, higher ground was northeast, so he needed to establish northeast. So Cliff ripped a small stick from a tree, stabbed it into the crack between sidewalk panels, and sat on his knees to wait.

For some reason watching the sun cast a shadow put a tune in his head. The baby back ribs song in fact. He hummed along. *I want my hmmm hmmm hmmm...* SHUT UP!!!! The end of the world was coming and all he could hear in his mind's ear was a song about ribs.

Suddenly a much bigger and more ominous shadow blocked out his sun stick, and he looked up from his knees at crotch level with a great big white horse. "Well, call me Wilbur..." Cliff said.

"Boy, there. Are you Kōno, Cliff?" A scratchy voice seemed to emanate from this muscular beast.

"Why yes I am. Are you Mr. Ed..."

"No. No one here is named Ed." From atop the ivory creature leaned a very old, yet surprisingly spry looking, bearded fellow with a crown on his head and a bow slung over his shoulder.

"If you're looking for the renaissance fair," Cliff quipped, "I'm pretty sure it's moved on to Maui, it was a limited engagement kinda thing."

"I am called Conquest. You are to be The Witness. I have come to collect you."

"Conquest?"

"Yes. Or Pestilence. Some of my friends call me that."

"You answer to Pestilence?"

"Surely."

"I'm going to call you Patience."

"No, Patience is a girl's name."

"No, Patience because you let your friends call you Pestilence. You must have a good heart... somewhere under all those wrinkles."

"What do you mean?"

"Well if my name was Cliffny Awesomesauce, and my friends came up to me and started calling me Chumpsicle Jones, I might not be friends with them very long. How do you get from Conquest to Pestilence anyway? Also, is that name Spanish?"

"You may call me Conquest then. I don't think we'll be friends."

"We could be, you barely know me."

"I get the feeling we wouldn't get along very well. You're very chatty."

"Maybe I'm just nervous. Maybe I should call you Jerk."

"Jerk?"

"Yes, Jerk."

"I don't appreciate that name very much."

"Oh but I appreciate your assumption that we couldn't be friends?"

"Maybe not."

"Definitely not. Now if you gave me a couple days to show you who I am, then I would understand if we were incompatible as amigos."

"You're right. That was rash. I'm sorry I disrespected you."

"Apology accepted. Now Mr. Conquest, what can I do for you?" Cliff glanced down at the stick impatiently trying to see if the shadow moved.

"No, it's just Conquest. Mr. Conquest was my father. Ha. Ha. Ha. Ha. Ha." His dry huffs that could almost be mistaken as a robot short-circuiting were contagious, and soon the two of them were rolling on the floor laughing. Even the horse giggled a little.

"Good one, Conquest!"

"Thanks. I didn't come up with that one."

"Nah, that one's about as old as you are. Hahahah! Get it?"

"I thought we were getting along. Why did you have to go and make ageist jokes?"

"I wasn't being ageist."

"Sure felt like it to me."

"Hey buddy, come on now. I didn't mean it. Just fooling with ya."

"Promise?" Conquest's scratchy voice took on a childlike quality.

"Come on, you're adorable who would wanna hurt your feelings?"

"Awww shucks."

"Hey buddy look though: it's getting pretty late. Your mom and dad are gonna be worried."

"You're right! I gotta get home!"

"Which way you heading, Conquest?"

"Hmmm." He didn't seem to remember what was happening. Why he came here. Who Cliff was. It was most convenient given the circumstances. "Where are we?" asked Conquest.

Cliff looked at his watch, it had been about ten minutes, he could work with that. "We're in Hawaii, kiddo."

"Hawaii... Pearl Harbor! That's where I'm going!"

"That's a little distance from here, you better get a move on!"

"Okay! Thanks for hanging out with me!"

"Anytime, Conquest. And don't let anyone call you "Pestilence." If they can't say anything nice, they shouldn't say anything at all. Remember that."

"Thanks!" Conquest rode off the way that Cliff had come with a smile and a wave, and when the horse's shadow cleared, the stick's shadow had moved some, and Cliff got his heading and once again sprinted off at full gallop before the Knight of Short Term Memory Loss remembered why he had come this way. Which didn't take long. Conquest stopped his horse about one hundred meters down the road and turned back to see his prey had escaped him again.

"Oh shit." He got on the horn, "Witness seen in proximity of the stadium. Set heading for northeast of Pearl Harbor. Use caution. His wits are unparalleled."

*****

After a bout of coughing and wheezing from exhaustive running, Cliff took another knee on the Kamehameha Highway. Per his estimates, he had a little less than twelve miles of walking in front of him. It was time to pace himself. If average walking pace is three miles per hour and he didn't stop moving, that would put him four more hours on his feet if he didn't tire. And he was already tired. The smell of roasting fast food by the base alongside burning flesh made him hungry. And confused. But mostly hungry. He could break route and find a restaurant to grab some chow, but he didn't want to find himself cornered in a crappy barbecue joint when the next ancient knight came to collect on him. His hands could be sticky. Wouldn't leave a very pretty corpse, *brisket*.

He decided to break off slightly back to the water to catch a fish. If his time on a boat taught him anything, it was that the water could be life giving as well as life taking. He hated that there was anything good to say about the Navy, but he needed lunch and his foot was getting a blister. He hobbled along the Pearl Harbor Bike Path in Neal Blaisdell Park and again sat down. This time next to the charred corpse of a fisherman holding a line already strung up. He grabbed the line, and luckily for him, the line already had a fish! This was turning out to be a great idea.

He reeled in the fish, clubbed it once in the head, and gutted it on the shore. He took off his shoes to air them out, and built a small fire using the fisherman's hat as fuel. Then he speared the fish with his knife and held it over the flames to cook. It took a little while, as the fire was pretty pitiful, but he was overjoyed to rest his legs. Cliff never fancied himself a runner. Especially not in Basic when he had to run a lot. The other recruits were faster, had more endurance, or maybe just faked it better, but Cliff frankly was over doing his best for people that didn't appreciate his efforts. He may as well have been called "24601" for all the Admirals cared. And because he couldn't be bothered improving for them, they couldn't be bothered giving him a break. They were in the most boring Mexican stand off one could surmise. If he did better, they'd still work him only to have him swab the decks. If he did worse, they'd still work him only to have him swab the decks. He had gone to college, but technically for communications. What the hell good was that now, he thought. If only he went to officers' school, he might be better off. On the other hand, all the officers he knew were at the bottom of the harbor.

As he took his first bite of his carbon-covered cod, in the distance he saw a familiar figure gliding across the water towards him. Unable to run far because of his feet, and without much cover around, he pried the jacket off of the fisherman and put it on as gently as he could so as to not tear its burnt fabric. He lifted the cooked corpse from the bank and put him on his lap and ducked his head down under the fisherman's long hippy hair. This time a fiery red horse stepped off of his cloud over the bay and onto dry land, where each step on the bike path was like a mini explosion between hoof and concrete.

"You there!" the man on the red horse called to Cliff. "You!"

"Me?" Cliff spoke from under the fisherman hoping he would get lucky again.

"Yes. Are you Kōno, Cliff?"

"Me? Why, no! I'm... a fisherman.... Named... uhh..."

"Speak up boy, your voice is muffled." The horse trotted closer and the rider called again, "Are you Kōno, Cliff?"

"I'm a fisherman. They call me... Fisher."

"What an apt name. I am looking for a man named Kōno, Cliff. Not to impugn your word, but can you offer some proof of your identity? He has already slipped past one of my rank with a measure of trickery. Do you have a driver's license? Or perhaps your fishing license?"

"Uhhh, I think so." Cliff reached his hand into the man's pockets and felt around for a wallet. After several attempts, he finally felt an abnormal lump in his shirt pocket and pulled it out. "Here it is!" Cliff chucked the wallet in the direction of the voice.

"How is your vision, Fisher?" The man dismounted his horse and stepped beside him, to pick up the wallet.

"Well it's been better, admittedly!" Cliff called from below the corpse. "Why?"

"You know you just threw a leather pouch of snuff?"

"Oh. Shoot. Wrong wallet! Haha!" Cliff continued to pat his pockets down, and finally found it in his back pocket. "Here it is... I think. By the way, who do I have the pleasure of speaking with?"

"My name is War." War picked up the real wallet and inspected the cards within.

"Your fishing license is expired. By the way, your name doesn't match your card. What does the name on your license say?" Cliff bit his lip. "I tell you. Damn kids! Am I right?"

"Sorry?"

"Yeah my kids have done this before. Changed my license with one of those joke ones from the gift shops."

"All of your cards bear the same name," War said sternly.

"Damn kids! They sure are determined... I told them Identity Theft was a crime. They just never listen. False documents, laminated this and that... those kids are sure gonna get a talking to."

"Why would they go to such lengths?"

"Well honestly they're my step kids. Bastards, all. They never much liked me, 'cause I told them they couldn't fish with me. They wanted the daddy bonding time, and I told them it was too sacred an activity to bring them, and they've been out to get me ever since."

"That sounds like a tall tale, Fisher. What's your last name? I'll have to check you in the system." Cliff was starting to sweat. Mostly from the weight of this slimy corpse, but also because this War guy was less stupid than Conquest.

"Uhhhhhh. Price."

War pulled the hand mic from his walkie-talkie up to his mouth. "This is War, putting out an APB for one Fisher Price, repeat, Fisher Price. Dispatch can you please confirm an identity?"

"This is dispatch," the walkie barked, "sending you the photo and information on Fisher Price now, War."

"Thanks, Rose, you're a peach."

Cliff sneezed and a burst of dust ejected from the fisherman's chest as though a mummy had been shot in the back.

"Gesundheit," War muttered barely looking.

"Danke," Cliff mumbled.

War's phone rang out, and he picked it up to examine the incoming info.

"Price?"

"Yes?"

"This doesn't look like you at all. This photo almost looks like a plastic quadruple amputee. You have limbs, Price."

"No, no, no, these are fake."

"Also this Fisher Price I'm looking at has normal skin color. Yours is all black and ashy."

"Exactly! This whole Pearl Harbor attack did this, burnt me up pretty good!"

"Why aren't you screaming in pain then? You don't look so hot."

"...I'm part Irish. We're used to burned skin."

"Ahh."

"So you've not seen a Kōno, Cliff then?" War asked losing hope.

"I haven't, as you pointed out, me vision ain't what it used to be."

"Fair enough. Well, sorry for the burn. If it weren't Armageddon, I'd call an ambulance but you'd end up paying a lot for not a lot I'm afraid with the time we have left here."

"You know, for a guy named "War," you're a damned respectable fellow."

"I'm trying, friend. I tell ya, I have three older sisters and my dad always wanted a boy to train as a fighter... but I wanted to go to art school. We settled for cop at the judgment of humanity, and I'm doing my damnedest."

"Your dad sounds just like my dad. Always telling me what to do. Maybe I didn't want to enlist, did he ever think of that?"

"Preach, Mr. Price. Preach."

With that, War climbed back on his horse and galloped northeast to find Cliff, just as Conquest suggested. After the sound of war hooves receded into the distance, Cliff crawled out from under the fisherman and took a bite of the fish.

"Damn. Cold."

*****

It was already passed midday and Cliff was getting nervous. Not too long ago he saw a ghost fly by and hurdle lightning bolts at neighboring housing complexes. An army of Mormons on horseback just eliminated anyone stuck in traffic on the Queen Liliuokalani Freeway. This end of the world stuff was starting to get old. Cliff swung his arms up and back to stretch out his shoulders which were getting tighter and tighter with every mile he put behind him. The one nice thing he had come to relish was the overwhelming silence that came with global extinction. He was waiting for his Henry Bemis moment—all the world was dead, finally time to read his books... what was gonna happen to ruin it?

And as if on cue, the sound of improperly inflated tires echoed along the highway at a slow crawl. Cliff turned to see who was coming, and sure enough, the next immortal plague upon him rolled up on two wheels, stopping about ten meters short.

"Hey," Cliff called.

"Hi," called the Segwayman.

"I like your gun."

"Thanks. It's a vintage Winchester."

"Gnarly bro."

"I thought so."

"I half expected your Segway to have a gun rack on it," Cliff quipped.

"I looked into it. It messes with the balance."

"Ahh of course, how could I be so silly?"

"Yeah, well. So you ready?"

"For?"

"You're The Witness. Kōno, Cliff. I saw your file."

"Tsk tsk tsk. Abductions without introductions, where did you learn kidnapping?"

"Well I'm Famine! Pleased to meet you!" Famine rolled over with his hand raised and high-fived Cliff before Segwaying back to his spot. "So... you ready? It's been a long day trying to find you."

Cliff didn't respond right away. He obviously couldn't outsmart this guy. He was alone on an elevated highway, nowhere to run or hide. Cliff tried to size Famine up. He was a skeleton with a gun, but frankly, had kind eyes. Though inherently Famine was his enemy. He couldn't sweet talk a guy who finds practical solutions to seemingly major problems, e.g. riding a Segway to work on Judgment Day.

"You win," Cliff called to him. A cold wind blew between them.

"Really? Just like that?"

"Just like that, Famine. By the way, you immortals need to read some parenting blogs. All of you have really devastating names. If my mom named me Famine, I'd prolly kill myself."

"It was a little tough."

"The kids call you Fammy?"

"No!"

"Ooohhh, touchy subject. Tell you what Fammy, my feet hurt from all the walking. Come pick me up on that contraption of yours, and let's go witness some shit."

"Time to Witness. The boys'll be so happy I found you! And don't call me *Fammy!*" Famine rolled with gusto to scoop up Cliff. With prisoner aboard, he spun around to drive back the way he'd come, but Cliff ripped the Winchester from Famine's shoulder and held it, rather awkwardly, pointed straight at the back of Famine's cranium.

"WHOA WHOA WHOA! Let's cool it here, Witness, let's take a deep breath..." Cliff cocked the rifle with one hand like a cowboy. "WHOAAAAAA! MERCY! Let's please slow our roles! What can we do to stop my skull from going splat? These things are bloody terrible to reconstruct!"

"You can turn your ass around, right now."

"Turning, roger that, no problem! Turning!"

"You don't need to narrate, Fammy. Just drive the damn machine," Cliff demanded. Famine subtly pressed a small panic button on the side of the handle, which lit up once bright red and then faded out. Famine grinned a little. *Backup's coming bro.*

"Not gonna lie, when I first saw you, I thought, 'This guy's gonna be real cool! He's Hawaiian, he looks like the Rock's pudgy cousin, he's got a Hawaiian shirt on'... which leads me to a question... if you wear a Hawaiian shirt in Hawaii, do you just call it a shirt?"

BANG! Cliff fired into the air, and ripped a hole in the sound barrier. The shot echoed for a hundred miles. "WHOAAA! I can't hear, I CAN'T HEAR! KŌNO?! CAN YOU HEAR ME?"

"Shut up bro, please, you're screaming."

"KŌNO? HELLO? I CAN'T HEAR!" Cliff pointed the barrel back at his skull. "OKAY OKAY! YOU'RE THE BOSS!" The Segway sped off up the road, eventually turning onto Komo Mai Drive.

*****

"SHOOBY DOOP, SHOOBY DOP, SHOBBY DOBBY DA DEEEEE DOP—RAMMA LAMMA BAMMA DEE DOP..." Famine scatted at the top of his lungs, still barely able to hear his own voice.

"I'm gonna pick the next song, Fammy. Sing me some Chumbawamba."

"SORRY I DON'T KNOW CHUMBAWAMBA. HOW 'BOUT CREED? I KNOW SOME CREED! DUN DUN DUN DUN DUN DUN DUN DUN..." Cliff pressed the barrel into Fammy's spinal column, interrupting the vocalized guitar build up. "ALRIGHT, NO CREED."

"What if we stop singing awhile? I'm getting a headache."

"YOU'RE THE BOSS, BOSS."

At a distance, the fourth horseman followed behind on his pale stallion. Whereas his peers before pursued Cliff with desperate exigency, the pale rider adopted a slightly more calm and calculated tactic. His horse sauntered leisurely, each step lighter than the last. The pale rider and his equine companion enjoyed the gentle breeze from the moderate pace of their pursuit.

As the Segway coasted up the street, it came to a cul de sac, but the dead end quickly transitioned to a footpath known as the Manana Trail. The Segway approached the steel gate separating the mountain hills from the neighborhood, and Famine waved his hand like a magician over the gate and it swung open. The two-wheeled contraption continued to roll on over rougher terrain with its skeletal captive and gun toting Navy man aboard.

167

"So Kōno, Cliff, what are your plans when we arrive wherever we're heading?"

"Not quite sure yet, Fammy. You weren't part of the plan when I cooked it up," Cliff sighed. "Sounds like your hearing is coming back, thank the lord."

"Haha no, I never lost it. But dammit was it funny watching you twitch."

"You're a riot, buddy, truly you are."

"Yeah, I was voted most likely to be a comedian in high school."

"How 'd that one turn out for you? Though I bet Halloween was really easy for you as a kid."

"Ha ha ha. Bravo, Navybeans."

"At least you drank enough milk, your bone density looks top notch from here."

"Funny you're so quick to discuss health and wellness, since when I found you, you were hobbling along like Jabba the Hutt's runaway nephew. You've really proven just how dependable the Segway is—perhaps I'll be investing in their stock hereafter."

"Why don't we cut the chit chat, Wishbone. Fact is, I'll blow your bloody dome all over the forest, and though organic material is good for growth, I get the feeling that you're about as good for nature as Exxon."

"Ooohh, topical. Now tell the one about gun control!"

"THAT'S FAR ENOUGH!" a voice tore through the canyon below the paths, and the Segway came to a stop. Cliff, taken wildly aback, grabbed hard onto Famine's body and repressed the rifle to his jaw.

"That wasn't you, was it Fammy?"

"I'm not so theatrical as that. You've known me for a little while now."

"Who's there?" Cliff called out, not seeing any faces in any direction around them. A patch of earth in front of Cliff and Fammy glowed red with heat, as the earth began to melt and bubble and eventually implode into itself revealing a dramatic sinkhole. Just as quick as the ground turned red, it turned an ashen gray and blew away in the wind. The face of a horse emerged from the hole, his eyes pupil-less, his mane salt and pepper. As it climbed forth, a figure on its back with sunken features and flowing white hair rode out. The pale stallion let out a cry like a banshee, and birds in the surrounding trees booked it like little bats out of hell.

"I take it you know each other?" Cliff said to break the ice at last.

"I am Death. Fourth Horseman of the Apocalypse. Strongest and smartest of all!" Death's voice reverberated off the plants and the path, shriveling up all life in its path. It even made Cliff's feeble mustache fall off—he'd been growing it for about a year! A cold wind swept over the path, and all goodness felt stripped from the world. Cliff shivered.

"Your name is Death too?"

"Pardon?"

"Well you have a vague resemblance, but how uncanny is it that I've met two demigod jackasses in one damn day, both named Death?"

"Ohhhhh."

"Go on?"

"You've met Death already?"

"Twice now. Hilarious."

"Did somebody call for *Death*?" another voice echoed on the air, and everyone looked up to see Death... the first one... floating to the ground, dressed in his classic Hollywood Reaper garb. "Oh, hello Famine. Death," said Death One.

"Death," replied Death Two glibly.

The three superhuman warriors stared at each other awkwardly, as Famine remained in a throat lock at gunpoint.

"Ok, please explain. What's the word on this one? Is *Death* like the biblical *Finn*? Like Michael and Jennifer were the year before, but Death was on the hot button list of trendy baby names when some sad mommy barfed you two schmucks out in the HMO baby ward?"

"Our dad liked boxing. He thought it would be great, like how George Foreman named all of his kids George," relented Death Two.

"*Our* dad? So you're brothers? How cute is that? So I take it you signed up for this because HGTV wasn't making another twin brothers renovation show?"

"Alright, take it easy. Leave the judgments to us, okay? You've been chosen as The Witness to the Apocalypse most foul by the Lord of All. Do you accept your mission?"

"What does this entail exactly lads? Is this because I missed jury duty a few times? The first time I moved and my mail got lost."

"You will ride alongside the Fearsome Five..."

"Starring Vin Diesel."

"...Shut up. You will ride and see the horrors of Judgment and before you sign the book of eternity yourself, you shall create the human account to be passed on should the world be born anew," explained Death One. "It's all here in this pamphlet." He handed Cliff a trifold glossy advert.

"*So You've Been Called as The Witness?: Ten Things To Consider Before the Judgment of Humanity*," read Cliff aloud. "I think I've read this before. Some guy gave it to me on the subway at Grand Central a few years ago."

"Please keep your thoughts to yourself. Read through it and decide," commanded Death One. "We'll wait." Cliff proceeded to read through the bullet points when Famine started to whistle. Cliff pushed the barrel harder into his skull.

"Oh right," Famine stopped.

"Did I miss anything?" asked the voice of War, who now sailed in over the trees and landed alongside the group. Conquest was right behind, and came to rest among them as well.

"You found him!" Conquest proclaimed.

"Yep," said Famine.

"Quiet please. Reading," said Cliff, annoyed with how chatty all the angels of destruction seemed to be. When he finished, he folded the pamphlet and considered his options. "So the way I see it... humanity is doneski. You've pretty much eliminated Honolulu already. You've likely torn through much of the rest of civilization. And the big guy upstairs has got his sights set on me, even though I'm a washed up kid from the Midwest. Is that pretty much the way of things?"

"More or less," agreed Conquest in his scratchy Don Quixote voice.

"Do I have any say?"

"You can have a last request, since the burden of the Human Tome lies in your fingers," said Death One.

"When this is all done. When I've seen the horrors, watched the despair unfold on infidels of all varieties. Once I've written the Tome... will you take me to the top of Mauna Kea on the big island? I want to watch the sun set one more time as the world burns."

Death One nodded.

"Okay. You win," Cliff sighed.

"Okay," Death One smiled. Cliff released Famine and the Five approached Cliff.

"Alright everyone. Hands in," Famine led the charge, vigorously slapping his hand in the middle of the circle. Conquest was next. Then War. Then Death Two, and Death One. Cliff sighed again, looking around at this rag tag bunch of intergalactic homicidal weirdoes and put his hand on top.

"Fearsome Six, on three," said Cliff. The Horsemen smiled.

"One, two, three,"

"Fearsome Six!" they all chanted together.

*****

War rode hearty and slaughtered villages on the plains and in the mountains with swipes from his terrifying fiery sword.

Conquest galloped atop his ancient steed, smiting the cities of the world with bolts of lightning from his bow, bombs and blasts at the brawlers, and chortled with the giddiness of an aged man who knew the punch line to a joke though he forgot its setup.

Famine segwayed between the islands of the world, devastating the scalawags with excessive drought and fire exhaled from his arid lungs.

Death Two glided among the forest nations and the river clans and snuffed the life force from all that remained like fragile embers in a vacuum.

And behind them all, Cliff rode on the back of Death One's horse watching all the calamity that befell his kinfolk, and for the first time in a long time, felt really sad for the people of the world. People that probably weren't innocent, or maybe even very nice. People that, given the opportunity, may have robbed him to get one foot ahead in life. Sure some were likely charming, and most probably cared for their kids and the friends of their towns, but all said and done, when these people were ashes on the terrain below, Cliff for the first time saw these people as one big family, all victim to tragedy and despair.

And even if his family wasn't very familial to him, he missed his parents back in Minnesota.

He missed his sometimes-sycophantic sisters.

And his little puppy that often peed on his rug.

He missed the bank tellers that always made him fill out deposit slips even though we should be passed that as a society.

He missed the old ladies on the bus that hocked up whatever terrors lay in their esophageal passages, only to swallow them back down to the depths to fester once more.

He missed his friends whom he fell off with, but especially his friends at the base. The Navy was a rough seven years for him, and there were only a handful of people that could stop him from doing something he may have regretted on any given day.

And they were gone. And he was all that was left in the world. Just Cliff. Cliff, and War, and Famine, and Conquest, and Deaths.

Cliff sat silently on the back of Death's horse and breathed deeply.

And after awhile, when his new associates had finished their work—when all humanity lie in collapse, and life itself was in thorough recession—after all these things, the world was utterly still. Like a tableau depicting the world to another type of sentient being. Cliff finished his chronicle in the Human Tome, and signed it. Then he and Deaths, War, and Famine and Conquest galloped across the sky from every corner of the globe in total silence to the crest of Mauna Kea on the big island in Hawaii.

*****

As the sun set for the last time over the ancient volcano, and the clouds danced in the wind below their feet, the Fearsome Six sat cross-legged on the rocks, and Famine pulled from his pouch a six-pack of some fine imported beer.

"Take one, pass it down," he said.

"Take one, pass it down," Death Two said.

"Take one, pass it down," Conquest said.

"Take one, pass it down," Death One said.

"Take one, pass it down," War said.

"Take one. Drink it down." Cliff held up his beer. "Gentlemen: today was a horrible...shitty day. People died, suffered, burnt up, yada yada yada. But you know what?" He made eye contact with each of his new friends.

"Today, despite it all... today I had meaning. And purpose. And agency. Today was the best day of my life." He nodded at each of them. "Cheers!"

"Cheers!" the Fearsome Six clinked their bottles together, and sipped their beers, and expelled some, "Ahhhhs," and watched the sun set for the last time on humanity.

Not a bad spot to watch the end of the world.

"La Cucaracha: Origins"

7:30pm New York Time, December 21, 2012 — Murray Hill, NYC

"**D**ay fifty-seven of Death Watch.

This morning, my adoring supporters, I made a discovery. Perhaps some of you have as well, in your hours of strife. After enough time meditating, and recollecting the joys of my life... seeing the sadness manifest in unique ways, like being in the grocery store and realizing I may never drink another overpriced organic carrot and ginger smoothie... seeing the bittersweet looks in my best friends and acquaintances lives... I finally had a moment when I opened my eyes today when I didn't feel alone. When I was... well, not happy, obviously... but okay. I was okay for the first time in fifty-seven days. Since my doctor reluctantly told me the x-ray showed a shadow on my lung, and that it was severe.

If you're a regular reader of mine, you've seen the range of emotions, you've seen the stress, and many of you likewise have seen the stresses in your own lives, with your own illnesses in various stages. I'm finally in a place where I'm okay to let go. My doctor left me a message this morning, not ten minutes after I finally discovered my peace, asking me to come in for one final assessment.

Ladies and gentlemen, readers and ramblers alike, may the remainder of your days be joyful, may you feel calm and peace, and may your pain gracefully recede as the suns set in your own lives. Thank you for being loyal readers. I couldn't have

*made it this far without you, and I am thankful for
each and every one of you. This shall be my last post.
I bid you adieu.*
  - Lucha Racha, la Cucaracha"

*****

"Good evening today, Lucha. You can have a seat,
the doctor will be with you shortly." Lucha stood at
the counter he found himself checking in at for almost
two months now.

"Thanks Rosario. Oh how was your weekend by
the way? You had that picnic with your kids right?"
Lucha and Rosario had come to be great friends, or at
least great acquaintances in the wake of his illness.
She was a lovely roach, with a great attitude that made
him feel safe whenever he came in.

"Oh that? We were supposed to have it on the
riverfront, but Steven had a racquetball thing that
came up and Stephany wanted to visit her dad
instead. So it was just Rusty and I. But it was a lovely
day."

"I'm sorry to hear they missed out, but I'm glad
you got to relax a little!"

"Me too, Mr. Racha. Thank you." She smiled a soft
and bittersweet smile and he reciprocated.

"Anytime, Ros."

Lucha sat down in his usual chair he'd come to
love. It was a crappy wooden chair, with a bit of black
pleather covering an irregular patch of cotton, which
peeked its little fibers through a tear on the left side.
But it was comfortable in that familiar way, if not in
the traditional way. The tinny sound of the tube TV
echoed from the far end of the room. There was no
video, just a little white dot in the middle emanating a

pathetic glow—the afterglow of its former glory—
seemed oddly appropriate given the locale: a waiting
room in the budget cancer ward in Murray Hill,
Manhattan. There were a few other roaches there,
some he'd seen regularly, including the bus lady from
the 1st avenue line and her four grandchildren. They
ran around on their six tiny legs like they were dogs or
something, playing with hand-me-downs of hand-me-
downs. You could see how much she wished she were
on a beach in her native Jamaica. But this is NYC: the
place everyone wants to go, except its residents. She
was stuck here for life.

Lucha pulled out a fitness magazine but the pages
were stuck together so he quickly gave up and
twiddled his thumbs. It won't be long. He breathed a
long sigh out and leaned back in his chair. And sure
enough, moments later, he was called into the small
doctors' room and asked to strip down and put on a
paper gown. The gowns were always changing.
Today's had patterns from Seurat paintings. Seemed
pretty ritzy—they were usually from half-rate
children's cartoons. He slumped his shoulders back
and sat back on his two upper hands when the doctor
came in.

"Good evening, Mr. Racha." The doctor was brimming
with excitement but didn't want to show it yet.

"Doc, I think we know each other well enough
now."

"Very well, Lucha…"

"This city, dammit. Can't we ever break down our
barriers and just be friends for Crustssakes?"

"You consider me a friend?" Dr. Waldorf asked,
taken off guard.

"I won't dignify that absurd question. You've given
me the most life changing news of my life. If we

weren't friends, I'd probably kill you." Lucha chuckled a little, and Dr. Waldorf echoed him, but with an air of hesitation.

"Well, Mr. Rach.... Lucha, Lucha... Lucha, I called you here today for a very specific and hopefully equally as life changing announcement today."

"Doc, I'm already dying, what else can you tell me?"

"Well that's just it, friend, you're not! I re-ran the blood cultures and asked for another opinion from an esteemed colleague and cancer specialist in town from Toronto for a conference. And it turns out the former diagnosis was a false positive!"

"...false...pos..."

"Yes! A false positive! You're not only not dying, you're going to live for a long long loooong time! It turned out the shadow we thought we saw was actually a calcification buildup along your bladder that essentially will act as a chest plate of armor, it'll be like your body is made of Kevlar! You're the only case of this I've ever seen, which is where the misdiagnosis arose from! How incredible, no?"

"Kevlar... chest plate."

"Yes, Kevlar! You're going to outlive us all!"

BANG!!! Right then, the roof of the hospital shook and crumbled. Dr. Waldorf quickly grabbed Lucha and dragged him from the room, and grabbed one of the bus lady's grandchildren as well, and the place evacuated in chaos.

"What the devil was that?!" someone screamed.

"Is that everyone? Did everyone get out??" Dr. Waldorf asked the group. "No! My son! He's still in one of the rooms!" a roach named Boach proclaimed. The doctor pulled off his lab coat and ran back in to grab the boy.

"What a hero!" the bus lady shouted to the now growing group of insects and insectoids outside of the collegiate medical facility. "Dr. Waldorf is a hero! He ran back to get some boy!" and everyone gasped, holding their jaws in anticipation.

Lucha meanwhile was numb. Paralyzed. Shocked. He waited with the others, unable to move in the wake of this news. After another explosion ripped through the building, and a cloud of dust and asbestos erupted from the main entrance, a silhouette of the bravest damn roach carrying not just the boy, but three boys and a cat, appeared in the doorway. All four coughed and wheezed as he put them down to the thunderous sound of applause. A news van had rolled up just a minute before and caught the brave doctor's daring rescue on tape. Some firefighters slid themselves under four of his shoulders and carried him away just in time from the now imploding husk of a medical facility. John Quiñroachés himself from ABC News appeared, and shook his hand, steering him away from the carnage.

With the blaze engulfing half a city block behind them, John asked him, "Dr. Waldorf, some may call you a hero, what would you say to them?"

"Oh John, you know, I'm no..." his humble statement was cut short, as he was tackled to the ground. The cameras tilted down to see a roach wearing only a Seurat-covered paper robe strangling the doctor.

"You told me I was dying! You told me I had two months! TWO MONTHS! You made me a liar to my fans! I'm a liar now! A safe and pathetic liar!!" The life was draining from Waldorf's eyes when the firefighters that pulled him from the blazing doorway grabbed his bottom feet and pulled him off, clunking his head on the uneven pavement. Quiñroachés following suit, picked him up by the back of his neck, as John was an enormous arthropod himself, and stared him dead in the eye.

"You defaced a brave American, and more importantly, a New Yorker. A hero in the eyes of millions. A doctor, a husband and father. Maybe even a grandfather. After he saved you! What have you to say for yourself, maggot!?"

Through gasps Lucha muttered, "Maggots are smaller, I take offense." Quiñroachés threw him to the ground, disgusted. "Scumbag. Traitor. You should scurry off now before I lose my temper."

"But he made me a liar!"

"Don't make me get angry!!" he puffed up his enormous body to double in size and his wings began to tear his fabulously tailored suit. Lucha knew he was beaten. He started to hobble away. "This isn't over, Doc!" As he departed, the roar of cheers again filled the air with the sounds of clapping and wings flapping via the fire truck's loudspeaker. "Hero! Hero! Hero! Hero!"

Several blocks away, Lucha noticed his foot had a cut in it from where he hit the curb. "Ow. Jerks!" He muttered a lot to himself as he limped to the nearest bar.

Through a crack in the brick wall, he entered La Piazza, a yuppy upscale pizza restaurant off of Third Avenue. As he sat on a stool waiting to be waited on, he looked up and saw the news was on, replaying the humiliating events that had just unfolded. Lucha looked for a remote to change the channel when the announcer's tone transformed to that of profound sadness; moments after the firefighters tried to put out the blaze, the structural integrity of the hospital failed and the building collapsed crushing everyone within a hundred feet. Which for a roach is the equivalent of an atomic bomb.

"Holy crap!!!!" Lucha stood up abruptly, knocking over his stool. No employees appeared to see about the ruckus, which occurred to him moments later. *Where are these jerks?* "Hello?" he hobbled around the counter and looked in the back. No one. He exited through the crack and purveyed the block. No one. Now that he thought about it, there weren't any helicopters, or sirens or horns honking, or profanities being shouted. There weren't any tweens tripping over their feet on the sidewalk, or deliverymen zipping by on their electric bikes. He scratched his head and weighed his options. His scalp was bleeding too he noticed. And he was getting light headed. "Well... dammit." He walked behind the counter and grabbed a slice and a napkin and exited.

Scarfing down the oblong piece of pizza, he went back to investigate the scene that revealed itself on the news. A touch nervous that Quiñroachés would still be there to assault him, and that the news was playing a trick, he snuck up behind pebbles and discarded soda cups, and alas! Nothing was left, but remnant chaos and destruction. It was like walking into Pompeii but with ugly skyscrapers in the background, everything ablaze, everything covered in gray dust and soot.

He sat on an old french fry and finished his slice. "Where's FEMA?" He continued pondering in silence for another hour. No one appeared, no soot was disturbed, everyone was gone. At one point he noticed a barge float passed him on the river, but it was also burning, and a blimp with news updates flashing sailed passed as well, bearing the ominous ticker:

Welcome to the End of Days, Repent and Fear as God is the Landlord of All, and Rent is Due!

Lucha was scared. And thirsty. The pizza was too salty. He climbed to his lower feet and limped around the neighborhood looking for anyone to explain what had happened, where everyone went, and why FEMA was nowhere to be seen—though he didn't hold out hope for that one.

He raided a deli of its sugary drinks and guzzled while he walked. Time slipped away, hours dissolved, the sun began to set and it began to get cold. And not just a little; it was around 30° that morning, now it was dancing in the single digits and trace snowflakes began falling all around. The sky darkened and fog began filling in the streets. He entered another establishment and huddled up in the corner. It was dank and soggy, just the way he liked it. But still, no customers occupied the space. And he began to cry.

"I can't believe it," he sobbed, breaking up each breath with a word to himself. "I can't believe I'm alone! And. everyone... everyone thinks I'm a fraud!" He tried to keep his composure but with no one around, what was the point.

A radio playing lightly in the background clicked on and off. He heard the static and ran to the kitchen where it was on the shelf. He pulled it down and tuned it a bit more accurately to AM 1010. Replays of the preceding days sputtered from the crappy deli radio transmitter.

"The apocalypse is nigh! Pearl Harbor has been demolished by physical and metaphysical forces. The Midwest has re-glacified, just as it had 10,000 years before. California has disconnected from the coast and worse, the surplus of actors that make up its majority have no life skills to survive the month. Bears from

Alaska have come down through the mountains and have begun opening karaoke cabins throughout the Rockies. The only remaining faction of survivors seems to be in the already unlivable New York City, in the Murray Hill neighborhood. A large flock of cylindrical tan creatures have been hopping and crawling through the streets and making their way towards the United Nations to hunker down as Nuclear Winter descends on the town that already struggles to keep the roads clear during regular winter. May God be with those poor tan creatures, and if you happen to be a survivor on the east coast, make your way to 42nd street: there lies the final outcrop of civilization as we know it." The radio cut out.

42nd street. The final outcrop of civilization. We are doomed.

Lucha tossed the radio to the side where it sputtered out its last blurbs and fizzled out like the rest of the world.

"Sasha!" he screamed. He hobble-bolted out the crack again and zoomed with all his might to the home he occupied with his cougar girlfriend and her pet "Guppy" the guppy—which was getting really big these days. It wasn't a puppy guppy anymore, when it stood up on its hind fins, it was about as tall as Lucha which got him nervous as he wasn't big on animals. Lucha much preferred his pet rock, "Rocky." But Sasha wasn't keen on inanimate pets. What do you do when you're trapped between a pet rock and a hard place? Out with the old, in with the enormous guppy. At least it was house-trained. The one downside to Rocky was he never made it outside before he had his little accidents so maybe Sasha was right.

As he crossed streets and braved the cold, these were the thoughts that crossed his mind. It struck him that he shouldn't be as worried about her guppy as her herself, but she tended to be very independent and Guppy tended to require a fresh water bowl so she was already ahead. Finally the familiar signs and landmarks of his neighborhood came into view and he knew he'd soon be nuzzling up with Sasha, eating leftover ravioli, and complaining that, "Dammit, Congress has really done it this time!" When he arrived, he kicked the front door in a grand gesture, but it didn't budge and he bruised his little toes. He gave it a slow shove, putting all his weight behind it and before he knew it, the door gave way with a quick thud, making just enough room to squeeze through but stopping short as debris from the falling building semi-barricaded the door.

"Sasha! I'm back, are you here!" He carefully navigated the fallen tiles and copper pipes that littered the shabby chic, but now more shabby than chic, studio apartment. There wasn't far to go, this was NYC after all, and within thirty seconds he knew what he feared all along: Guppy was gone. Also Sasha too. Now don't get me wrong, he loved his cougar girlfriend, but she was a force of a woman and since she was more... we'll say, experienced... than he, she tended to solve all problems without his input or conjecture. She was a doer. This started when she was a little roach still running around day camp in Hell's Kitchen. She majored in engineering in school and went on to be the first roach in space as part of NASA's program to test animal endurance in the vacuum of the cosmos. She not only excelled in that program, she went on to grace the cover of "Women Weekly." She was a celeb in her own right, and knew that enduring outside the International Space Station meant she could endure just about anything. So long story short, she was less than impressed with Lucha's art history degree from CUNY. Again they were in love, but maybe more in the way that you were inspired by your soccer teammate's innate ability and wanted to share a pizza than in the conventional male-female-Hollywood paradigm that plagued humanity since Clark Gable told Vivien Leigh to shove it. Though she was as desirable as both of them in their respective heydays. Lucha felt like Vivien after she was dumped, but always.

"Sasha?" No answer. She was gone. Or out. But likely gone, given the circumstances. He sat on his dust-covered ottoman that squeaked because of its clear plastic coating. It was uncomfortable and unpleasant. And he was sad. She was his rock—not to be confused with Rocky—and she was lost to him. The sounds of the cool and cooling wind tore through the place like the Colorado River cut through his stone façade. He was alone. Not just now, but in this world. His parents had died many years before—one from gout and the other from a broken heart. His brother Laramie was in the army. Last he heard from him he was in Liechtenstein or some god-forsaken country— he was probably dead as well. Guppy was a wimp, he'd never survive this, which left just his Sasha, and where was she? Just as likely dead as running for Empress of the desolate America that seemed to be left. Yes, he was alone.

He thought as he sat on that terrible ottoman, about what to do, where to go, if to go or if to do. What was left of him but a husk of a man? And since roaches are mostly husks to begin with he wasn't much before he was nothing. He tried to whistle to distract himself but he was never very good at it. This place was depressing. Dr. Waldorf's words echoed in his mind: "You'll outlive us all!"

Dammit, Dr. Waldorf! I don't want that! Then it occurred to him: *I don't want that.* What a brilliant and utterly simple solution! *I don't want that. I can change this. I can stop my suffering. But how?* He grabbed his blue racquetball and bounced it as he exited the apartment to ponder how best to kill himself.

After a couple steps the ball smacked into a crossbeam and rolled under the debris and he sighed and kept walking till the sting of the cold air infiltrated his lungs and he shivered. *The first real thing I do in my life and it's suicide. I don't even have the Internet to cheer me on.* He breathed deeply and watched his breath create a surprisingly beautiful cloud of life that floated and dissipated, and he felt poetic in his self-loathing. Then in the distance he noticed movement and it startled him. He ducked under a shrub and stared in that direction for a long time till it moved again. He only saw the edges of whatever the hell it was, but it was there and whatever it was, it was alive. He held his breath, which felt especially cold and unpleasant in his lungs, so he let it out with a gasp but tried to stifle the sound. The figure moved again and again, till it made a break for it and took off in a northbound trajectory. Lucha had to follow. There was still plenty of time to kill himself.

He kept his head low but tried to see what he was following. It was brown or tan, or even khaki, but shadows grew and shifted and it was hard to see. Then it dawned on him that perhaps it was one of the creatures he heard about on the radio. The one's heading to... the UN! The final outcrop of civilization! He could be saved, and this was his ticket to redemption! After all, roaches aren't tan and definitely not khaki, maybe these creatures, whoever they are, don't read cancer blogs or watch the news.

It had already dropped below zero. He double-timed his pursuit, but made sure to be subtle as he did. The one thing he learned from detective films was if you're tailing a guy keep at least a car's length distance between you two. He kept two car lengths. It helped that he already gathered where this poor fellow was going. His insights made him feel like the lion hunting its prey, and that gave him a glimmer of hope that maybe he wasn't as inadequate as Sasha inadvertently made him feel. He was Predator. Though he didn't see the second half of the movie, he assumed it was a successful hunt for that dreadlocked alien with the heart of gold and blood of a lightning bug. "Yes, I am the Predator," he repeatedly whispered to himself between shiver spells. "I'm coming for you Arnold."

Now this was a long distance to travel for a small roach like Lucha and the strange tan creature, and after three days and nights of toughing some of the worst temperatures any New Yorker can endure, he finally spotted the dozens of flags surrounding the enormous United Nations compound. It was like seeing Oz for the first time, and thank the lord: all the tourists were dead! He sat on the outskirts and watched the tan man hop up to the gates and jump right on through.

Now running straight in after him was risky, and Lucha hated the idea of walking all the way here and getting shot. Waste of exercise. So he snuck up behind pebbles and discarded soda cups, and after a time decided it was safe to proceed cautiously. He walked under the gate that the human giants erected to keep each other out and was so proud to stand under the Hunger Games flag at long last! That noble Mockingjay spread its wings across the light-blue backdrop, and inspired a hundred nations to attack Kiefer Sutherland's dad's house. What an awe-inspiring sight!

Lucha crawled under a crack in the security door and reveled at the enormous gray arches with blinking lights at their apex. A sign read, 'security entrance, please empty your pockets and remove your sweaters.' Well, security was gone, so he was leaving his sweater on, thank you very much. He continued into the main courtyard, and took a few moments to enjoy the statues that had been placed there in years passed. The globe with the cracks in it, the pistol with the twisted barrel. A child eating a Snickers. Actually the last one turned out to be a tourist caught in the flash freeze, but it was majestic nonetheless. He moved onwards, as the wind was starting to become unbearable.

Squeezing through a tighter crack in the main entrance he spied several tan creatures with UN hats and polos on, and with great trepidation approached the more portly fellow of the group.

"Excuse me sir?" he attempted as politely as he could.

"Who goes there!?" the portly guard shouted pulling his sidearm from his belt and firing twice in the air. Lucha hit the deck and covered his head, cowering in the entranceway. The tan creatures hopped over and surrounded him. He didn't dare look at them. The portly fellow held his pistol at arms length and said very deliberately, "You, there. You're that cancer liar who hates America and children!" It's amazing how quickly Lucha went from fear to rage, but as he stood up to give the tan man a sock in the tooth, everything went dark with a pain in the back of his neck.

When he awoke he was awaiting trial in a cell in the basement of the UN. Though this place would be terrible to anyone else, his people traditionally preferred these soggy dark prison-y environments. There were remnants of fecal matter on the floor; there was mold on the walls... it was like New Orleans! He loved New Orleans. As he gorged himself on the miscellaneous stains from the walls, a raspy voice came from the other side of the bars. He stopped suddenly as he couldn't quite make out the word. "Who's there?"

"My name is Blinky. I'm the King of the UN in the wake of Nuclear Winter."

"Blinky? What kind of name is Blinky? Especially for a King?" Lucha giggled to himself as he shoveled another bite of excrement.

"...It's a very common name, a strong name in fact. For my people," stated the voice in a now defensive tone.

"Pshhhh. Blinky. Well, King-that-sounds-like-a-pony's-name, who are your people?" He swallowed a gulp of green goo from a crack in the rock.

"We are the Twinkie clan from the North," Blinky stepped from the shadows into the light, and sure enough he wasn't tan, he was a golden god of corn byproducts.

"Twinkies? With the delicious white goo inside?"

"Delicious?! Have you eaten the sacred organs of my people?" His voice bounced off of the stone walls and the sounds of reinforcements grew louder as they entered the dank hallway.

"I didn't say 'delicious!' No no, I said 'precious! And definitely not edible!'"

"Are you sure, filthy arthropod? It sounded strikingly like *delicious!*"

"Respectfully, King Blinky the Twinkie, I don't want to talk smack about your hearing or suggest your ancestors are amazing treats, but perhaps you should have a checkup with your royal audiologist because I'm definitely not one to insult Canadian royalty, with that many angry soldiers standing immediately behind him."

"Very well then, heathen. Perhaps you did not."

A young guard stepped forward and tapped the King on the shoulder.

"Who dares touch my sacred shoulder?!" Blinky started again in a rage.

"Your Holiness, forgive me, but this fat ugly creature is the same one that told a bunch of cancer-ridden blog readers he was dying, but he wasn't... and also tried to assault John Quiñroachés from ABC News."

"You did what?"

"Me?" Lucha was terrified and livid that people keep bringing that up. "No, I was misled! That quack at the hospital told me I had two months; if anything I'm the mouthpiece for his propaganda! You know what they say about killing the messenger?"

"Yes, I do!" said King Blinky the Twinkie, "We must kill the messenger!"

"That's not what they say!" retorted Lucha.

"I'm pretty certain that is what they say!" Blinky shot back.

"Well for that matter, King, who is 'they' and what gives them any authority to say anything? After all, 'they' is a vague pronoun; at least with he/she/it you can point to whom that refers, but *they*? *They* can be forty-five people from a variety of backgrounds and levels of qualification."

"Shut up now, Fat and Ugly, that's enough from you!"

"Hey! Respectfully, King, that's pretty rude of you to just start calling me names. I at least asked your name!"

"What is your name, Liar?"

"There it is again..."

"What is your name?" King Blinky rolled his eyes, growing impatient.

"Lucha Racha."

"Well Lucha Racha, the fat and ugly lying cucaracha. Since you are worried about dignity, the sentence for your crimes..."

"Alleged!"

"Alleged crimes... you shall henceforth be known as... "Don." By stripping your given name, you are cast out from your tribe! Furthermore you are sentenced to death. And I insist you write an apology letter to Quiñroachés first."

"Why does everyone love this guy so much? Yes he's charismatic..."

"Enough! Guards!" The barred door was opened, and Lucha was forcibly chained up and dragged from his surprisingly snack-filled cell.

The Twinkie guards carried him to the throne room and locked him to a central stanchion where he had to bend awkwardly to accommodate the shape of the post. This was bad. It bothered him that in his last moments on Earth that he was having flashbacks to his days in camp oh so long ago when he was initiated into the boys' club in much the same way. Though at least that was just a paddling, and not whatever means these dessert devils used to execute their prisoners. He prayed for a quick and dignified death, like a beheading or a lethal injection... but death was taking its sweet time getting there. He remained bent over for the better part of an hour while a horde of Twinkie men, women, and children filed into the throne room to take their seats to witness the execution. His lower back was cramping, and these chains were cold. *Maybe their tradition demands death by old age.*

"Pssst." Lucha called to a nearby guard, who after two or three promptings finally walked over.

"What?" The guard asked impatiently.

"Firstly, you need to work on your bedside manor." The guard sighed and turned away. "Wait, wait, wait, okay that wasn't a great way to start." The guard returned reluctantly, and again asked, "What is it?"

"Two questions: one, how are they going to kill me? And B) will it be soon, because this is not a comfortable place to wait forever."

"Two answers: you will be burned alive, as is the custom of the Twinkie nation."

"Why is that the custom?"

"The greatest fear of any pastry is to be burned, idiot. Don't interrupt."

"Makes sense. Sorry."

"It's okay. I'm just trying to answer your questions, you can at least listen to me."

"You're right that was rude of me."

"Apology accepted."

"Thanks."

"Where were we?"

"Ummm. You know... I forget now."

"...me too."

"That's so weird right? We were just talking about this."

"This is why interrupting is frowned upon."

"Well it's obviously inefficient."

"Inefficient and rude."

"Fine, I get it, I'm rude, I'm rude; can you stop calling me names please?"

"It's not a name, it's an adjective. Oh! I remember, we were talking about the executioner."

"That's it! Right, when is he coming?"

"He's on his way."

"Do you have an ETA on that guy or what?"

"I'm just a guard. They tell me where to stand and who to salute, and that's pretty much it."

"Who would know?"

"The execution coordinator. His name is Stanley."

"Can you ask Stanley for me? I wouldn't be so demanding, but my back is really starting to kill me."

"Too bad it isn't really. Save us taxpayer dollars, am I right?"

The guard went for a high-five but Lucha remained chained and was forced to leave him hanging. The guard realized this after a moment, and completed the high-five himself. "No, I can't ask Stanley, unfortunately. He sees to lots of executions, so he's somewhere on the compound running around. We won't see him till he comes in right before yours."

"Does he have an assistant?"

"That's a silly question. What good is an execution coordinator without an assistant?"

"...not very good?"

"That's what I think."

"Does the assistant have a phone or a pager or something?"

"Again, I'm just a guard. You're barking up the wrong tree here. Though if it helps, they tend to do these kinds of executions on the hour, so it's quarter till now. So it'll likely be in about fifteen minutes. That's just a guess."

"I'll take an educated guess when I can get one."

"There you go!"

"Thank you... sorry I didn't ask your name... maybe I am rude."

"No it's quite alright, the commander doesn't know my name either, he calls me 13."

"That's kind of ominous, what an unlucky number."

"Yeah I'd prefer another number, but what are you going to do?"

"So what's your name?"

"My name is Curtis."

"Curtis, it's a pleasure to meet you. My name is Lucha."

"Lucha! I love that name."

"You do? Everyone always told me it was a girl's name."

"Typical. People are jerks. It's obviously a strong man's name. It's got a bit of ethnic flair. Just like my name!"

"Well Curtis isn't exactly ethn... right it's a very strong ethnic name..."

"We're like the black sheep brothers. That would be a great band name if you weren't short for this world."

"I don't play an instrument."

"You could learn."

"I suppose I could."

"The best thing about the Apocalypse is there's unlimited time to become anything you ever wanted."

"Curtis, I admire your optimism."

"And I admire your calm in the face of untimely death."

"Well let's just agree that we're both pretty cool."

"Agreed. All right, I'd love to keep chatting but the room is almost full and I don't want to look like I'm fraternizing. They withhold rations for fraternizing."

"That's fair."

"Well Lucha, see you on the other side."

"Yep, sounds good. Curtis, stay fly."

"I feel young, hearing you say that."

"Look, one more request. Maybe I'm over stepping my bounds here, but you don't have some Advil do you? My back is really uncomfortable, and if they're going to burn me alive, Advil won't really slow that down, but it might make leading up to it a little better."

"I don't have any. Too bad my wife's not here, she always carries some. But wait a minute, you mean because you're bent over?"

"Exactly."

"You know these pillars are adjustable? They need to accommodate a range of different sized criminals so there's a button that you push in here and it slides up and down." Curtis pushed it in and slid it up to its maximum height. "How's that?"

"Wow, that's so much better!"

"Glad to help! Alright see ya later!" He took a step back and shouted so everyone could hear him, "Death to the Traitor!" and without skipping a beat the crowd of golden onlookers repeated, "Death to the Traitor!" Even Lucha felt inspired, "Death to the Traitor" he said to himself before he remembered that was him. "Wait..."

Fifteen minutes came and went. Lucha began to feel crazy. He had been counting down seconds in his head, so when he got to eighteen minutes he scowled a little wondering if he was counting too fast, or if he skipped some digits. He was baffled. He looked up at the royal clock on the wall over the illuminated exit light and sure enough, it was several minutes passed the hour.

"Well anytime now I guess."

Another hour passed. The room had gotten testy. Having been cold when they entered, by now their communal body heat had steamed up the throne room more than a few degrees and the stickiness was becoming unpleasant, especially for the very young and very old. In fact one old woman fainted in the top row and was carried out. Several kids started crying and their parents tried to entertain them with various colorful toys they kept on their persons, but the fact of the matter was this was not the quick death he had expected it to be.

Suddenly the doors opened and a cold rush of air whooshed in, to everyone's relief.

"Who's ready for a murder!?" The executioner was all grins and raised his hands over his head to the delight of the audience. They cheered and stood to applaud him. The executioner walked over to Lucha and patted him hard on the head with a thunk. The kids burst into laughter, and the executioner laughed right with them.

"Your murder gown is inside out," Lucha whispered loudly, and the executioner realized he was right. He tucked in his tag and hoped no one else noticed, before picking up the torch from in front of the throne and kneeling in anticipation.

King Blinky entered the throne room and everyone grew quiet. He hopped to his chair and sat to the synchronized sound of the crowd sitting as well.

"We come here today, to witness the execution of this traitor who stands before us in chains and shame. After his pathetic life as a loser, and his momentary missteps as a citizen, it is my pleasure to declare that his flickering flame be snuffed out and hurtled from our city limits like yesterday's recycling. Mr. Johnson, please step forward."

The executioner stood, torch in hand, and approached the King. "Good Mr. Johnson, you are tasked with purging the life of this heathen and all around scrappy chump before us. Are you willing to do your duty in the presence of this noble mob?"

"It would be my honor as a proud member of the royal court and citizen of the Twinkie nation."

"Well then by the authority vested in me by the patriarchy, you may now execute your duty."

"So let it be done!" With those words the crowd erupted into a fit of cheers and Mr. Johnson the royal executioner turned to Lucha. He hopped to him and asked, "Do you have any final words, filthy creature?"

"Yes. Firstly, that's racist. You don't even know me, how can you call me filthy? Secondly..."

"I've heard enough." Mr. Johnson dropped the torch onto the pyre and within seconds the pile of tinder erupted into a gradual flame that ebbed and flowed in the wind still coming in from the throne room door by the glowing exit sign.

"Will someone please close that door?" Everyone hesitated.

"Someone, please, anyone? I don't care who it is." Two or three guards at once jumped to close it, but their simultaneous movements made them again hesitate, as no one wanted to look silly.

"Okay, stop, you three, stop. You're idiots. Just get in line." They lowered their heads with humiliation and rejoined their ranks. "You!" Mr. Johnson pointed at Curtis. "You make sure the door is closed."

"Me sir?"

"Jesus, close the door!"

Curtis quickly rushed to the entrance and slammed it with a loud thud that echoed through the chamber.

"Sorry, it's not as heavy as it looks."

"Shut up boy, back in line."

"Yessir." Curtis rejoined his ranks, and smiled slightly. He was appointed that great task. He couldn't wait to tell his mom that night.

The fire finally picked up some steam and engulfed the pyre. After a few moments it burned out. Maybe the twigs were a bit wet from the weather, or maybe there was a more divine intervention, but suffice it to say, when the ashes fell, Lucha let out a great cough and asked with the whole of his strength, "Does anyone have a glass of water? My throat is..." he coughed again, "full of soot."

A great gasp was heard throughout the room. The guards lowered their spears. King Blinky descended from his throne and approached the roach.

"You there, boy!"

Lucha looked around the room for anyone to bring him the water.

"BOY!" the King bellowed. Lucha looked up startled.

"Me?"

"Yes you, didn't I call you boy and look at you?"

"Well, there are about two dozen boys sitting between me and you right now, so it could have been anyone."

"What magic do you use?"

"What magic? I don't follow."

"You stood atop the mountain of incendiaries only to emerge unharmed."

"Unharmed is not the word I'd use, what with my throat... unharmed? UNHARMED! I'm alive??" It suddenly occurred to him that he hadn't burnt up as he thought. "HOLY CRAP!"

"Holy crap indeed!" saith the King with a look of utter displeasure. He stood under the prisoner and examined the scene. The wood was burnt through; the pillar was blackened with carbon gases. Even the prisoner himself was blackened but there were no signs of deformity or molten skin flakes. "Boy, are you aligned with the devil?"

"The devil? No, but officially I am a hockey fan and I grew up in Newark..."

"Do you ever say anything that isn't tedious? Seriously!"

"That's a hurtful thing to say."

"Mr. Johnson!" King Blinky beckoned the executioner to his side and pulled him in. "Any ideas here? We can't just let him go, and I'll be damned if he's gonna rot in our cells. I don't want roaches here; once you get one, the rest follow."

The executioner was at a loss. He breathed loudly to fill the air, then said, "Ahh uhhh... this is a tough one. I've never seen that before. Should we cut off his head? That has a certain circus-y appeal to it. Gotta have that flair or else the crowds spend less at the gift shop on the way out... we did a focus group and results concluded..."

"Shut up. Do it."

"Great!"

Blinky turned to the crowd. "This Sorcerer before us has withstood our fire! But what is a snake without its head?!"

The crowd cheered. Usually executions were over in thirty minutes or less, this was a special day!

"Reset the pillar!" The King returned to his seat and Mr. Johnson and his coordinator and the assistant pushed the fired wood out of the way and restaged a beheading. The pillar was lowered to the size when Lucha was first strapped in and his back immediately cramped again. When the stage was set, the coordinator reached out to the assistant who passed him his espresso, and the two retreated to their desk on the other side of the room to let the executioner do his job.

Mr. Johnson picked up the gratuitously oversized ax and approached Lucha. "Do you have any final words... umm.... prisoner that may or may not be filthy depending on your hygiene?"

"That's not much better than filthy, dude. Ya ever think I'm dirty because you threw me in your motel-grade prison system? That's right I said it, your staff did a bad job tidying up. If I had access to Yelp, you'd get quite the rating."

"Any last words, man? Don't draw this out."

"Yes. I am ready to die. I'm not proud, but knowing that I stood tall when everything else was dead makes me proud. Guppy, mommy, daddy, maybe Laramie, possibly Sasha, the rest... I'll see you soon. To anyone I've wronged, I am sorry! That's all."

Mr. Johnson nodded and shoved Lucha's head onto the chopping block. Lucha breathed his last deep breath on Earth and let it out with a long sigh.

Freedom was in sight. He closed his eyes. The roar of the crowd receded into the background of his mind and a subtle calm overtook his body in a way only a monk could reproduce. Zen was his, and peace was coming. He envisioned his tombstone, "Here lies Lucha Racha, la Cucaracha. Proud man, beloved son and brother, owned a pet in New York despite its limitations. Faced death with the grace of a cabbie staring down the Long Island Expressway during rush hour. Prince of Princes." With that, he felt a feeling on the back of his neck and knew it was done. Then moments later, felt another feeling. Then another. The zen receded and the thought crawled into his mind, I wonder why swift death feels like I'm getting battered at a Groupon'ed massage parlor...

The silence rushed away and he heard the crowd screaming. He opened his eyes and saw a couple neck scales on the ground but heard Mr. Johnson swinging and hacking to no avail. He rolled over and watched in terror as the ax fell at him. He shut his eyes forcefully and felt another whack but it didn't hurt. He reopened his eyes and looked at the panting Mr. Johnson, who had dropped his ax to catch his breath. Lucha sat up and the shouts stopped. He looked around the throne room and all eyes were wide and on him. He had survived again! Everyone was in shock.

"Guards!!" King Blinky shrieked and a dozen uniformed Twinkies came and removed him from the block. "Secure the prisoner. Counsel meeting right now, huddle up!"

Guards surrounded Lucha, and the crowd booed, realizing this could be a bust. Some slowly filtered from the bleachers set up for this event. As Mr. Johnson rightly predicted, this was a slow day for the gift shop.

How did I survive? Twice!! Then the refrain from Dr. Waldorf came back like a song stuck in his head: "You'll outlive us all!" *Could this be true?* He said Lucha had a chest plate of calcification. Chest plates—no matter how strong—don't burn-proof bodies, and don't ax-proof necks. Maybe the calcification spread? Was he invincible? He raised his hands in the blocks to look at them. They felt heavier than usual. And as he stared ever closer, he could see little white micro particles growing under his partially translucent skin. It's true! He'd soon be un-killable!

*****

The King paced back and forth in the throne room, bouncing his racquetball, while his advisors debated ways to murder this seemingly helpless-yet-invincible cucaracha. He refused to make another attempt that might fail in front of the crowds. These events were how they determined who was fit to rule. If they saw another survival, well, he could kiss the re-election bid goodbye. That was out of the question.

"What if we poison the boy!?" said the eldest advisor.

"Poison is not dramatic! You think we'll win hearts while he slowly craps his pants to death in front of the gentlewomen of our people? Also what makes you think if he survives a burning and a decapitation, he won't survive a little arsenic?" the youngest advisor retorted.

"Does anyone know how to drive those peacekeeping trucks we have in the garage level? We could tie him up and run him over?" suggested another.

"That would be dramatic and very visual. But how can we be sure this will work?"

"Agreed," interjected Blinky, "I like where your head is at, but we need to know this works. We can't risk a debacle with the East River Pipeline vote next week. The press will eat us alive."

"Only if it fails," clarified the unsuccessful executioner, Mr. Johnson. "How do we guarantee it won't?"

The oldest advisor flipped his dentures in his mouth as he often did when he was weighing tough decisions. "We could consult a doctor? They could analyze him and see where his weak spots are."

"That could work!" shouted Blinky, "Brilliant, old friend!"

"Thank you, Your Majesty!"

"Johnson, get Dr. Blinky on the phone."

"Yessir!" The ambitious young scamp grabbed the portable phone from its throne-side charger and pressed speakerphone, then dialed the royal doctor's office.

"You have reached Dr. Blinky's office, Upper East Side. Our business hours are..."

Johnson replaced the phone on its charger.

"Well that was great. What the hell are we doing here? This is preposterous." Blinky said.

"Wait, Sire, didn't your wife go to medical school?" asked the eldest advisor.

"She did! Send for the Queen!" three or four guards sitting on the periphery, stood to find her, but all hesitated as each rose simultaneously and no one wanted to look silly.

"Jesus," sighed the King. "You! Get my Queen over here immediately, tell her to do a full work up on that dumb idiot."

"Yessir!" said Curtis, saluting proudly. He scurried from the room.

*****

The Queen arrived at once, and Curtis unlatched Lucha and sat him down for inspection. The Queen pulled out her bag of instruments. While she examined this and tested that, Curtis and Lucha discussed music in a whisper, and Curtis told him all about how he wanted to be a jazz bassist before his mother sadly informed him that they could never afford such a prestigious instrument or the lessons therein. She bought him a tin whistle, knowing it wouldn't be the same but at least he could start understanding sheet music and getting his hand-eye coordination in order. So he played and played endlessly throughout his childhood and still practices today when he can.

"Curtis, would you mind getting your whistle and playing me a song? I'm afraid. And it would calm me some I think."

"It would be my honor! And lucky for you..." Curtis removed from a pouch on his side the disassembled tin whistle.

"Your Majesty, the prisoner requests a song. Would it be okay to play one while the examination takes place?"

"Good idea. The crowds are getting restless anyway. Get on with it."

He screwed the pieces together and asked Lucha for a request.

"God, who knows... what do you play?"

"I like jazz still, even if I never got my bass."

"Lovely."

Curtis put the whistle to his lips, licking them just so, and began playing a down tempo version of My Favorite Things by John Coltrane. It was extremely moving hearing the emotion in each note. The high-pitched tones reverberated beautifully off of the immense stone fortress that caged Lucha. After the fourteen minute rendition had concluded, Lucha wiped a tear from his face. The Queen too. She finished her analysis as the song finished. It was lovely. Proof, even, that hope and love were still alive in the world. Without another word, Curtis disassembled the whistle and replaced it on his belt. The Queen joined her husband at his side on the far side of the room.

"Thank you," Lucha whispered to Curtis, and wiped another tear.

"Well what did you find?!" bellowed the pastry King to his much more charming wife. She plopped her bag of tools on the round conference table.

"I found a lot."

"Perfect!" the King rubbed his hands maniacally.

"And you're not going to like it."

"What do you mean?"

"Well," she bit her lip; "He's got advancing internal and external ossification, so basically there's a thorough buildup of calcium surrounding the whole of his body. It's a rare condition known as Fibrodysplasia ossificans progressiva. Even his soft roach organs are coated in the stuff, but surprisingly inside and out it's more like a bulletproof body suit. This is unique; I've never seen a case like this. He might as well be a dragon, because you won't penetrate his body."

"...So what do you suggest?" asked the King, again losing his mind with anger.

"For dragons, you could always steal their gold..."

"How do we kill him?"

"The long and the short of it is I don't know. Old age might work?"

"Get out!" he stood and screamed like a maniac.

"I'll be in the library." She left calmly.

"We need to do something drastic. Johnson!"

"Yessir?"

"The bottom several floors of this facility are bombproof correct?"

"So they say, yes."

"Good, gather the crowds and assemble them on the other side of the bomb-proof glass in the subbasement. Tonight there will be fireworks if it kills me."

*****

The sun set through the haze of nuclear winter and what light was left faded from the narrow window behind the throne. He moaned in his shackles, longing to die, wishing it could be at his own hand. He tried to whistle Curtis' song but his whistling was terrible so he hummed to himself, when a new class of guard appeared to take him from the throne room. A dark robed figure with a rifle and his accompanying teammates entered the room and beckoned for him to follow. No one spoke, no one needed to. *They figured out what to do. I'll soon have release, and be with my family.*

The rifle-laden soldiers escorted him down a series of corridors and stairwells until he found himself in the center of a vast silo with a warhead dangling from the ceiling like a deadly chandelier. The door slammed behind him, and he looked up through the bombproof glass overhead at the many men, women, and children who had come earlier to watch his demise and were now filing into the witness chamber. The smallest children waved sparklers and had giant foam hands with "#1" written on them. Some of the men had face paint on as though they were watching a football game. *Maybe the gift shop did okay after all.*

Over the loud speaker, a familiar voice blared with some feedback asking him, "Do you have any final words, Creature-with-whom-we-have-many-differences-and-may-be-unhygienic-but-given-time-and-resources-could-prove-clean-after-all?"

"I like that best of all so far. No. No words. Hasta la vista, respective babies." He lowered his head, closed his eyes, and smiled softly knowing that this would be over soon. He had once again come to full terms, just as he had on day 57 of deathwatch. The Zen he felt in the blogosphere had wrapped itself around him like a blanket. He was warm at last. Soon he'd be home.

King Blinky grabbed the microphone from Mr. Johnson. "Ladies and gentlemen, boys and girls of all ages—I proudly present you with the main event: the execution of the Twinkie nation's most formidable enemy. Death be upon you, cucaracha!"

A countdown clock appeared over the amphitheater glass starting at ten seconds. The crowd counted down—*nine-eight-seven...*—while the two generals adjacent stood by with their keys securely pressed into the launch computer. *Three-two-one!* The keys pivoted in their place and a flash of white burst instantly.

Five minutes later, the energy from the blast calmed down, the explosion began to settle. Despite thick coughs and messed up eardrums, things began to clear up again. Whiteness diminished, an audible ringing reverberated like Coltrane in the throne room. Lucha opened his eyes. He was on the floor of the silo, and the silo was demolished. Everything was destroyed. Everything. The bombproof glass was not bombproof but rather fire resistant as the warhead is supposed to launch the opposite direction, spouting its propellant into that chamber. The entire compound was ash and nothingness. The United Nations was a crater with one sole survivor—a particularly tough cucaracha.

Lucha looked around and rubbed his ears. He was submerged in a hole the size of the empire state building with no way to climb out as the walls had been blasted smooth to the point that Lucha's usually prehensile fingers couldn't grip even a nub. He examined his body. The carbon from the failed-burning-at-the-stake was blasted clean; the scar tissue that surrounded his neck was blasted smooth. In fact, he'd never looked better. *Talk about a chemical peel.* And once again, he was all alone. This realization struck him like an atom bomb—you will outlive us all! Everyone. All of us. Every last person.

This was like a curse: may you outlive us all. And he knew he would. With no semblance of mystery or majesty. He'd never explore the ruins of Egypt or see the castles of India. He'd never have kids to teach his philosophies, he'd never get a guppy puppy and name him "Guppy Two." He'd never try falafel, or engage in a super spicy eating contest in Coney Island. He would be here at the bottom of this silo. Alone. In the dark of nuclear winter. Cold and shivering.

And he did outlive us all.

Epilogue:

"Yokte Yok, Guess Who's Back?"

December 25, 2012 — United Nations, Manhattan, NYC

L ucha huddled in the corner of the silo wishing he had a slice of pizza to drown his sorrows when the ground began to vibrate ever so subtly. He assumed it was his stomach at first, but it continued and grew in intensity over time. Then stopped.

Lucha figured his cabin fever had kicked in and decided to just ignore it. He was a friend of some homeless guys in his former life and anytime they made a big deal about strange observations, they found themselves carted off by the cops. Not that there were any cops left: those frosty tarts saw to that.

No! They weren't Pop Tarts. Pop Tarts can't take over society! They're prone to cracking under pressure. It was the Twinkie clan! The term "tart" can have more than one meaning—a Twinkie can be a tart, just like a Pop Tart can be a dancer. Never paying attention. Oyy.

The ground started to rumble again, so Lucha tried to hum-sing a little.

"The ants go hmmm hmmm hmmm hmmm hmmm, hurrah hurrahhh.

The ants hmmm hmmm hmmm hmmm hmmm hmmm, hurrah! Hurrah!

The hmmmm hmmm ants go hmmmm hmm hmmmm, the little one hmmms all over her face, and and we'll all feel gay when Johnny comes marching home."

His song was a bit off key and the words were mostly wrong, but one couldn't exactly tell because the rumbling at this point had gotten so severe that

Lucha was starting to think it wasn't just his mental faculties crumbling like the walls of Jericho. But just to be sure....

THE ANTS GO HMMM HMMM HMMM HMMM HMMM...

A giant flash above the silo lit up the desolate sky and he was now mostly pretty sure he wasn't off his rocker.

"So what the hell then?" Lucha tried to scuttle himself up the wall to see, but the surface was still too slippery like the dozens of other times he tried to escape. Something about fusion reactions makes the walls like Teflon... *if only there was society still, that'd be a great business,* he thought to himself.

The sky opened up above the silo and what looked like intergalactic warships came in through the flanking clouds.

"Whoa!" he said, falling on his exoskeleton. He rolled himself upright and stuck his face to the small crack in the wall adjacent and watched as the dozen ships hovered about ten meters over the ground before making a soft landing in the debris. After a moment, a panel door on the ship opened, with the sound of a fresh jar of tomato sauce breaking the seal. Several armed men wearing almost no protective clothes, but with dazzling jewelry and headdresses exited the ship with spears at the ready to attack.

They surveyed the area around the ship and then the one with the most festive headdress whistled back to the ship. Three more men dressed similarly came down the ramp with another man behind them. It was hard to see much of him, except that he was taller and tanner, and his teeth seemed to shine like a pop star.

"All clear, sir!" The whistler told the man in the middle.

"Good. Thank you. So where are we exactly?"

"According to our charts, it's a town called 'Murray Hill.'"

"Well, where's the hill?"

The armed men spun around in all directions. One spoke up.

"I think it's that, sir." He pointed at a gradual slope that one of the roads made going north and south.

"That's the Murray Hill? What a pathetic thing to name a town after."

"Well it's more of a neighborhood I think, God King."

"And the town?"

"Manhattan. New York."

"Oh good! We made it after all. Where's this Broad Way I've been hearing so much about?"

"Uhh..." the whistler consulted his maps, "looks like a few kilometers west of here."

"Not bad, not bad. Anyone up to head over and dig through the remnants of the *Wicked* prop room tonight? Maybe hit Sardi's after for a bite?"

The men sort of nodded and looked around at each other.

"I'm not big on musical theater but I can eat."

"Very well. Any survivors that you're aware of?" The God King asked.

"Uhh..." the whistler consulted his scanner, "looks like one, faint one very nearby."

"Hello?" the God King called out beyond their circle. "Have your spears ready, gents, but also, smile! We don't want to scare the natives." The circle of warriors gripped their obsidian-tipped weapons tighter, but all flashed their pearly whites as the God King commanded.

"Hello? Is anyone out here?"

Lucha squinted at the men through the crack in the wall.

"Hello!" he shouted back. His voice echoed up through the silo, creating an ominous roar and the warriors jumped, as they spun towards the silo.

"Who said that?" the God King called, nervously.

"My name is Lucha! I'm the sole survivor."

"Where are you?"

"In the silo. Come over!"

"Why don't you come over here? We'll wait."

"No! You must come here."

The whistler pulled out a small pocket edition of "The Art of War."

"God King sir, Sun Tzu would not advise going into that silo. He says, 'the worst policy of all is to besiege walled cities.'"

"What would Mr. Tzu advise?"

"Well, he says the skillful leader subdues the enemy's troops without any fighting."

"Uh huh? And how does he advise we proceed?"

"I haven't finished the book yet. It's very long."

"Okay, great. Thanks for the advice. I'll take it from here."

The God King stepped ahead of the warriors.

"Lucha is your name?"

"Yes."

"Hey Lucha, my name is Bolon."

"Your name is Colon? That's like one of those Freakonomics things!"

"No Bolon, BOLON. With a 'B'."

"Like, that's so rap money, BALLIN'!"

"I don't think this is working the way we'd like, come on out and we'll chat face to face. What say you?"

"I'm trapped, I can't come out."

"Dammit Lucha, why didn't you say that in the first place?"

The God King snapped his fingers and two men ran back into the ship and flew above the silo.

"Yep, he's in there, sir," the pilot said looking at the debris below.

Bolon spoke into his communicator, "Pull him out then, let's get on with this."

A long rope dropped out of the ship and landed at Lucha's feet. He quickly scuttled up the rope and the ship landed once again beside the crumbling silo. The door opened and Lucha exited the ship and came to the side of Bolon and his warriors. *They were freaking tall!*

"Bolon?" Lucha asked.

"That's me," Bolon pushed his underling out of the way and knelt down to speak to the little cockroach.

"Bolon Yokte is my name."

"Is that Dutch?" Lucha held out his hand and shook Bolon's finger.

"No. I'm from the Kingdom of the Maya. I'm kind of their god. In fact, you should probably call me God King."

"No kidding?" Lucha nodded. "What the hell are you doing here then? Glad you came along obviously, but man, this place is a dump!"

"Ahh never underestimate a place. A little elbow grease...any town can be a fixer upper. Any leaders around we can speak to?"

"I guess just me! You can call me Mayor Lucha."

"Well Mayor Lucha, we want to settle here."

"Sorry. Again great to have you, but remind me. What's so great about here?"

"This is New York."

"Uh huh."

"Most expensive housing in the country."

"Uh huh."

"And no one's left."

"Uh huh."

"What's not to get here, little Mayor?"

"The part where you flew across galaxies to come to New York I guess."

"Not galaxies; the Mayan Kingdom is in Mexico."

"Woof. Didn't know that. What are the Maya doing about the Narco problem?"

"Not our concern. Everyone's dead."

"Oh right. Right."

"But now we are here, and we want to settle here."

"Ok." They stared at each other for a moment in silence. "And what am I supposed to do about it?" Lucha asked finally.

"Well how much for a two bedroom with a patio on the water? Preferably a doorman building. I know doormen are probably all dead, but I like that desk in the lobby."

"Uh... I mean an apartment on the water is stupid expensive... you're talking about like 4 or 5,000 big ones a month. For a two bedroom."

"Right. Before. But now that there's no demand, how can you help me out on that one? I got a lot of people interested in premium real estate."

"Let me get this straight. You, Bolon Yokte, God King of the Mayans, got in a spaceship and flew international during Armageddon to get a better deal on rent?"

"Yep." Again the "Mayor" and the God King stood for a moment of silence.

"Well, Mr. God King Yokte, I think today's the start of a beautiful friendship!"

Epilogue: "Yokte Yok, Guess Who's Back?"

ABOUT THE AUTHOR

Born and raised in Chicago, IL, Michael went on to New York University's Tisch School of the Arts and graduated with a BFA in Film & Television Production and a Minor in Philosophy. He is the co-founder of New York City based AireBedd Productions—a full service video production company that create dynamic web and branding videos, as well as music videos and short films.

"La Cucaracha & Other Tales of Apocalyptic Revelry" is Michael's first book. While he doesn't believe in brimstone and Armageddon in the conventional sense, he is a Cubs fan... And just because the Cubs won the World Series a few years too late for this story, doesn't mean the fabric of space time isn't actually already tearing as we speak.

Build your bunkers. Time is short.

WHERE TO FIND HIM

www.michaeldominguezbeddome.com

You can find Michael on social media at:

facebook.com/MichaelDominguezBeddomeAuthor

twitter.com/mickeybedroom

instagram.com/mickeybedroom

plus.google.com/+MichaelDominguezBeddome

pinterest.com/mickeybedroom

amazon.com/author/michaeldominguezbeddome

Note From the Author:

Reviews are gold to authors! If you've enjoyed this book, would you consider rating it and reviewing it on www.Amazon.com/dp/B06XF7BWL8?

ABOUT THE ILLUSTRATOR

Kevin Budnik is a Cartoonist and Illustrator from Chicago. He is the author of several collections of autobiographical comics. Find his work at kevinbudnik.com.

www.ingramcontent.com/pod-product-compliance
Lightning Source LLC
Chambersburg PA
CBHW051243250626
47155CB00009B/3143